PROMISE KEEPER

ALSO BY MARY FREMONT SCHOENECKER

Four Summers Waiting
Finding Fiona - Maine Shore Chronicles
Moonglade - Maine Shore Chronicles

MAINE SHORE CHRONICLES

Promise Keeper

Mary Fremont Schoenecker

FIVE STAR

A part of Gale, Cengage Learning

GALE
CENGAGE Learning™

Detroit • New York • San Francisco • New Haven, Conn • Waterville, Maine • London

GALE
CENGAGE Learning

LIBRARY OF CONGRESS CATALOGING-IN-PUBLICATION DATA

Schoenecker, Mary Fremont.
    Promise keeper : Maine shore chronicles / Mary Fremont Schoenecker. — 1st ed.
        p. cm.
    ISBN-13: 978-1-4328-2537-9 (hardcover)
    ISBN-10: 1-4328-2537-2 (hardcover)
    1. Art thefts—Fiction. 2. Domestic fiction. 3. Government investigators—Fiction. 4. Clairvoyants—Fiction. 5. Maine—Fiction. 6. Florida—Fiction. I. Title.
    PS3619.C4493P76 2011
    813'.6—dc22   2011025022

First Edition. First Printing: October 2011.
Published in 2011 in conjunction with Tekno Books.

Printed in the United States of America
1 2 3 4 5 6 7 15 14 13 12 11

This book is dedicated to the Lemieux and Fremont families, my inspiration for the Maine Shore Chronicles.

CHAPTER ONE

Biddeford, Maine
2008
The pungent smell of leaf mold and piney earth hung in the air over a newly dug grave. A woman glanced at the hole, shuddered and hurried on. Weak spring sunlight cast a shadow over a nearby granite headstone. The woman stopped in the headstone's shadow and stooped to make the sign of the cross over the inscription on a small marble marker beneath it:

Julie Margaret Donovan ~ rests with angels ~ 5-15-2007

Tears welled as her eyes rose to the headstone.

Julie Fontaine ~ beloved wife and mother ~ 1958–2004 RIP

She reached to trace the inscription on the granite stone, kissed her fingers and bent low to place them on the infant's name. *"Dieu benisént,"* she whispered, "God bless." Taking a long-stemmed yellow rose from her tote, she laid it on Julie Margaret's marker. Named after its deceased maternal grandmother, the child was also the woman's namesake—Margaret. Baby Julie Margaret held a special place in Margaret Chamberlaine's heart.

She stepped away from the grave to look west toward the older section of Good Shepherd Cemetery. Clumps of frozen, gritty snow still banded graves set beneath evergreen trees standing sentinel.

Pulling the collar of her wool coat up around her ears, Margaret quickened her pace across the brown grass until she

7

reached the stone that marked the grave of her husband.

"You would not understand, *mon chèrie*, but I must do this for Jacques. I will be safe in God's hands, as you are, my Jean."

While her fingers brushed across the stone's inscription, a vision rose in her mind, and with it came tears. *Fishermen huddled on a wharf, trying in vain to shield her husband's lifeless body from her eyes.* Nine years had passed since a fierce spring storm battered Jean's boat and claimed his life.

Margaret's whispered prayers, and the wind whistling through the pines were the only sounds in the graveyard. She shivered, reached into her tote and placed the last yellow rose before hurrying away from Good Shepherd Cemetery, her short, plump figure casting a fleeting shadow on the stones.

Clare couldn't keep shock out of her voice. "What do you mean you're going to be out at Francois's Fancy for a couple of weeks, maybe longer? I can't believe my ears. You, who rarely ventures away from this side of town. What's gotten into you?"

"What's gotten into me is God's justice. I'm going to do whatever it takes to achieve that for the Fontaines."

While Margaret packed a suitcase, Clare paced the floor in her *Tante*'s bedroom. Dark haired and full bosomed, like Margaret, Clare usually displayed the persona of a calm-natured nurse, but she could also be as formidable as her surrogate mother.

"I think there's more to this than you're telling me. What exactly has Jacques asked of you?"

Margaret closed her eyes and took a deep breath. "In the first place, I promised to help out at Francois's Fancy for a few weeks because his wife is away. Jacques says Kathleen is staying with her *tante* in Chicago. The old woman is on her deathbed, and God knows when Kathleen will be back." Margaret stopped to cock an eyebrow at Clare. "My dear friend Jacques asked if I would help with the meals and be there for Jacques Paul, if he needs me."

Clare shook her head. "I don't get it. I mean, I know they need someone to cook for them out there, but what possible help could you be to Paul—"

She stopped pacing suddenly and smacked her forehead with her palm. "Oh, Lord, *Tante*. No. Not again! I can't believe Paul would even consider asking you."

"Asking me!" Margaret threw her shoulders back and pointed a finger at Clare. "You are forgetting, my Clare, a time when it was very important that I help your Sergeant Remi with an investigation. I was reluctant to do so for many reasons. It was my *grandmére* who was the seer, not me, and I hardly knew Remi Windspirit. Paul, Jacques and Madelaine are like family. I could never refuse to help them. Jacques Fontaine has been like a papa to you since my Jean died. You should know that better than anyone, Clare Margaret!"

Clare sank down on *Tante*'s bed, braced her elbows on her knees to hold her head in her hands. *Serious stuff is coming when she calls me Clare Margaret.*

"Lord knows I'm being selfish here, but I simply don't want to go through the worry of you being in harm's way again."

Clare realized that this time she was *questioning* her surrogate mother's use of psychic powers instead of *requesting* it. Experience had been a good teacher. She wanted no repeat of the head injury that Margaret received at the hand of a killer in an investigation gone wild—Remi's investigation.

Francois's Fancy at Biddeford Pool

The soft buzz of the alarm clock interrupted his dream. Paul Fontaine's eyes opened to pale yellow light slanting through the shutters and spilling onto the pine floor.

"Damn it. Why can't she get it through her head that I want

9

sunlight and the sound of the sea coming through the window?" A voice in his head spoke. *Won't happen. Not with Kathleen.*

He reached to turn off the alarm and a sharp pain sliced through his thigh—a warning that he couldn't twist his body that way . . . no twisting, or prolonged strain on that leg were the words of the surgeon who repaired Paul's shattered hip bone with pins and screws.

Paul's helplessness left him testy and irritable, especially where Kathleen Murphy Fontaine was concerned. His father married the young widow three years ago, but Paul still found it difficult to accept Kathleen's presence at Francois's Fancy. Hell, he found it difficult that *he* should be here in this house once again, dependent upon his father.

He rubbed his hands over his face. Glancing at the bedside clock, his eyes settled on a small framed photo on the nightstand. He reached for it, carefully, this time. His mother's face stared back at him. She was waving from the deck of *Julie's Dream*. Her wind-blown chestnut hair a sun-kissed halo, in sharp contrast to the white sails billowing behind her.

Paul's thoughts jarred at the sound of heavy footsteps on the stairs. He put the photo back and eased his injured leg slowly to the edge of the bed. Pushing with his elbows he rose up, slid both legs over the edge, easing his left leg to the floor.

Seconds ticked by after a light knock before the door opened. Paul squeezed his eyes shut, willing himself to be stoic.

"Good morning, Paul."

"Mornin', Pa. If I could see out the window, I might know whether it really is a good morning."

If Jacques Fontaine caught the sarcasm in his son's voice, he gave no indication. He went to the window, guessing that Kathleen had probably closed the blinds before she left. He threw open the shutters. "Little chilly for May, so I won't raise the window till you're dressed."

"Whatever." Paul said. "I need to get to the john."

Jacques looked around the room. Paul's jeans hung over the arm of his easy chair, a T-shirt draped over the ottoman in front of it. He opened a dresser drawer and tossed a sweatshirt to the chair. "You'll need something warm for the porch. I'll help, if you wish, when you come back from the bathroom."

Jacques leaned his shoulder for Paul to grab for balance. "Ready?"

"Paul leaned heavily on his father's shoulder with one hand. He struggled to rise and hobble out of the bedroom without his cane. "Got to cut out the drinks, Pa. My bladder is full to bustin'."

Jacques's mouth quirked in a grin. "Ah, yes, doctor's orders to force fluids. It's good you're following orders. When you finish in the bathroom, I've got things set up on the porch for breakfast this morning. Margaret is coming."

"Margaret is coming?" Paul repeated, searching his memory. Suddenly he smiled. *Kathleen left, and we need Tante Margaret.* "I forgot for a minute, but that's good, Pa. It gives me a reason to go downstairs. *Tante* always shares a little hope, and God knows I need it. Besides which, she's a hell of a cook. Is she bringing anything?"

Jacques chuckled and shook his head. "I told her just to bring herself, but you know Margaret. She'll probably bring enough food for a week." Jacques closed the bathroom door. "Holler if you need me. I'll wait in your room."

Memories came rushing as Jacques stepped back into Paul's bedroom. He rarely came into Maddy's or Paul's rooms after Julie died. Paul had asked to have his room left just as it was when he left for his job in New York.

Never know when you need a port in the storm, he'd said.

How prophetic, Jacques thought. *Three weeks have passed and Paul is just beginning to move about without help.* He swallowed hard, his gaze fixed on a painting at the far end of the room. His first wife's paintings still lined the walls of the house, and memories of her lined his heart. The years could not erase the memories.

The painting was of the dune ridge in front of Francois's Fancy. At the end of the sea path, Paul and Maddy were building a castle in the rose-sparkled sand. Julie captured it all . . . everything the children loved when they came to live at Grandpa Frank's house by the sea. Julie had named the house Francois's Fancy.

Jacques knew his children found it hard to accept Kathleen in this house. He should have sold the place and moved after Julie died, but he couldn't bear to leave Biddeford Pool. He walked to the window with the portrait in hand, looked out to sea, then closely again at the painting. Paul's skinny, suntanned body knelt beside his sister, his small hands molding the sand. Maddy, chestnut hair falling over her face, was the image of her mother. Jacques sighed. *How Julie would have loved it that Madelaine was a mother—*

"Ready, Pa?"

Startled out of his reverie, Jacques hastily put the painting back and turned to help Paul.

Margaret Chamberlaine leaned back in a porch rocker. "It's a glorious day, eh, Jacques Paul? Before you know it, you'll be setting up your easel on the beach again."

"*Tante,* you are the proverbial optimist. I'm afraid my thoughts are not on painting."

"But they should be. You are an artist. One of the sisters at the Retreat Center gave a wonderful definition of art. She was talking about creativity, and she said 'the root meaning of art is to fit together.' We do this every day, *mon chérie.* When we fit things together we are creating, like when I put ingredients together to bake a cake, and you mix your paints to create a painting, eh? You create beautiful pictures, Jacques Paul. And I make delicious cakes!" *Tante* threw her hands up in a familiar gesture as she rose to pour more coffee.

Paul shrugged, smiling, and reached out to squeeze her arm.

Jacques could see that Margaret's simple example affected Paul. "She's right, son. You do need to focus on art. You're getting stronger every day, and Cornerstone Gallery needs you."

Paul closed his eyes and drew a deep breath. A muscle twitched in his jaw. "Pa, I know that. I have been trying to figure out the best approach to the gallery. Contrary to what you may think, a bullet in the hip did not affect my brain. I have not been lying upstairs in la-la land from painkillers."

"I never thought that, son."

"I keep trying to remember something that might have led to the break-in. I've relived that day at the gallery over and over. Every blasted detail I gave to the cops. I've even tried to pinpoint something in the weeks before it happened, like maybe there was a weird visitor to the gallery or a strange inquiry from a patron." *What keep's coming up is Suzanne, and I'm sure as hell not airing that relationship—yet.*

Margaret rose to take their plates to the wicker tea cart that Jacques had wheeled to the porch. "I'll leave you to chitchat while I get started making chowder for lunch," she said.

"Worries go down better with soup, eh?"

Jacques jumped up to hold the door open for her.

"You're a sweetheart, Auntie Mame," Paul called.

Margaret turned to beam a smile at him. "Sharing the housework makes it easier to share the love, *mais oui?*"

Jacques sank onto the cushioned wicker settee next to his son. "You haven't heard anything about the gallery this week, have you?"

"No, but I'm sure Boston is pulling the strings. The endowment for the gallery came from Sean Rafferty, you know. He's literally the owner."

Jacques nodded, remaining quiet for a few seconds. "You remember my colleague, Professor Williams, from the art department? He's the one who bought *Sunrise at the Wildlife Refuge* from your first show at the gallery."

"Sure, I remember him. Why?"

"He told me there is an Art Lost Register Company in New York City that has a huge data base to track stolen art."

Paul knew his father was trying to be helpful, so he tried to keep an edge from his reply. "You forget, Pa, that I worked in New York and I'm familiar with the Register. I've been out of the investigation since the robbery, but I'm sure Cornerstone's owner or the police have been in touch with New York. They've just not notified me of much progress."

CHAPTER TWO

Clare dialed Maddy's cell phone, a picture of Maddy and Patrick forming in her mind. "Hi, babe. Am I interrupting anything?"

Maddy laughed. "Heavens, no. Patrick thought I could use a break after last week, so he went fishing today."

Last week? Last week was the third week in May. . . . Clare gasped with the sudden understanding that she had forgotten the anniversary of baby Julie's death. Usually *Tante* reminded her of those things, but with all that's been going on with Paul and Papa Jacques, she must have forgotten.

"Geez, Mad, how stupid of me. I feel really bad that I forgot. I haven't an excuse for not remembering Julie Margaret. I can't blame the ER, though my shifts have been rotten lately. Full-moon madness and late-spring storms—it's been a zoo! I should have been there for you."

"It's okay, CeCe. It's better I deal with it quietly and move on. That's what Papa tells me. Only thing is, he doesn't understand the Irish. The Donovans have Irish hearts that never forget. Patrick hasn't a clue how to rescue himself from sadness, but he tries to be very supportive of me, just like Papa always is."

"Your dad is one of the reasons I called you. Did you know that *Tante* is at his house for the next week or two?"

"Out at the Pool? How come?"

"*Tante* to the rescue, I guess, but I was as surprised as you. I

15

just found out that she was invited because Kathleen left for Chicago. You did know that Kathleen was leaving?"

"Yes, she mentioned she would be away taking care of an aunt who is dying. Strange thing is, I don't remember my dad telling me when she was actually leaving. I guess he thinks I'm too tied down at school to ask for my help out there. I know Paul needs moral support as well as physical help since the gallery disaster, but he hasn't asked for me, either."

"I know, babe. We've been down that road with Paul, remember?"

"How can I forget? You've always been there when I needed you, Cec." Maddy chuckled. "Thick and thin, eh? Seriously, though, are you working tonight?"

"No, I just finished the early shift. Why?"

"Why don't you see if Remi will come here with you and Paul for a drink, and we'll all go out to dinner. We need to talk."

Paul sat against pillows on the broad window seat in the den, his leg propped up on an afghan. He looked up at his mother's paintings adorning the walls, at his father's bookshelves filled with history collections. All successful images.

His mind spinning, he stared at his mother's painting stool, but the image he saw was not Julie. It was Suzanne, long raven hair brushing against white breasts. Naked. That was the way East Village artists painted her. "The money paid for my books, last year of college," she'd said. "The less I had to depend on my father, the better." He shook his head and flicked that image away. She never did explain why she didn't want to depend on her father.

Peppering all his thoughts and everything he had observed that day were the clouded memories of Suzanne. Even in his sleep she replaced the usual nightmare of the shooting. He wanted to believe that she cared about him. She said she did, but the question remained: why hadn't she called? Not one word since—

"So, here you are, *chéri.* Your papa left for an appointment at the university. He said you might be in here." Margaret set a plate of cookies and a cup of tea on a small tray table and carried it to the window seat. "Your leg is better today, eh?"

"You're going to spoil me, *Tante,* but yes, it feels better propped up like this. I came in here to make a few phone calls, but then I remembered curling up here to watch my mom paint." Paul patted the cushion and smiled up at Margaret. "The window seat became too inviting."

"Your mama was a beautiful artist, and you inherited her genes, *oui?*"

"Maybe so, but I'll never achieve what she did. I think my destiny is to live through a bunch of disasters that follow small successes."

"No, no, Jacques Paul." Margaret walked around Jacques's desk, ran her fingers over the desktop and flopped into his swivel chair. "Your first showing at the gallery was a big success, and the next year they made you director, right?"

"They made me *interim* director after the new director died suddenly of a heart attack. As Patrick Donovan would say, 'that's a bit o' luck, *mechushla.*' "

Margaret tried to hide her smile by shuffling papers and tidying up Jacques's desk. "Don't sell yourself short, Jacques Paul. You must be qualified for that job. You studied for a degree at the university, no?"

Paul closed his eyes and nodded slowly. He was being distracted by issues he didn't want to talk about. Margaret wasn't an easy woman to deal with, what with her cryptic predictions and psychic mind.

"A degree in art history is only good in large cities where you can make contacts. I was lucky to be hired as associate curator of the Modern Art Museum in New York, but the money went down the tube with the recession in my first year on the job. Last one in was first one out, and we have disaster number one."

Paul swung his leg off the window seat. "The only reason I got lucky in Portland was because no one qualified had been interviewed since the director died. I'm holding on like I know what I'm doing for the past six months, and out of the blue a thief gets in and steals a priceless painting from under my nose."

Tante fired up a wordless prayer for courage. She pointed her finger at Paul. "Enough about successes and disasters. Fame is a windy thing. Your papa told me about the phone call from Florida. You need to get your wits about you, Jacques Paul. Regroup, eh? You should be down there, in Sarasota." The words were out of her mouth before she considered them.

Paul looked at her with mixed emotions. *God, how she manages to get straight to the heart of the matter.* "I was about to work on that, *Tante,* but convincing the gallery's benefactor that I should play sleuth is not going to be easy. He's keeping a pretty good rein on proceedings, from what I hear."

"What do you know about this man, er, this benefactor?"

"Only that he's a lawyer and a philanthropist. He has worldwide connections according to those in the know. Old money from Boston. He's donated to many institutions in the area, the old mill project where Patrick is, for one. Pa told me he gave big-time to the school you attended in the old days, *Tante.*"

They exchanged a look, and Margaret sent back the hint of a smile. "I don't mind being reminded that it was the 'old days,' and, yes, I went there when the place was a Catholic boarding school for girls. I wasn't a boarder, you understand. The sisters let me be a student because my papa did all the carpentry work in the chapel for free. More importantly, Jacques Paul, tell me, is this man . . . this benefactor, would his name be Sean Michael Rafferty?"

"Well, yeah!" Paul said, unable to keep the surprise from his face. He reached for his cane and stood. "Don't tell me you know him?"

"Eh, sort of. When you said he gave money to the school, you triggered my memory. I believe Mr. Rafferty's daughter went to the school long after me. I never knew her, but I learned later that she died when she was a very young woman."

Margaret's gaze stopped at the photo of Jacques's daughter, Maddy, on the desk. "Mr. Rafferty gave a big endowment to the school in his daughter's name and since the school closed, he continues to give gifts every year to the nuns at the center. Sister Agatha told me all about him. There is a plaque in the chapel with his name on it."

Paul leaned heavily on his cane, making his way to the desk. "Very interesting. He sounds more approachable than I thought." He kissed Margaret's cheek. "You've given me the incentive I need, Auntie Mame. Maybe I'll make a call to Mr. Sean Rafferty."

Margaret rose as Paul came around the desk. They were both startled when the phone rang.

"Fontaine residence," Paul answered. Immediately, surprise and concern mingled on his face. Margaret heard his hesitant reply. "Yes, I'm Paul." He looked quizzically at Margaret. "Yes, she's here." He listened for what seemed a long time before he said, "Of course, we'll wait. Yes, thank you."

Paul sank into his father's swivel chair, swiped his hand over his face and opened his palm toward Margaret in a pleading gesture. "I can't believe this is happening. That was one of the security staff at the university. Pa found the dead body of a student in the foyer outside his office. He collapsed on the spot, and they called us because he refuses to be taken to the hospital."

"Collapsed?" Margaret's fingers flew to her lips. *"Mon Dieu!"*

"One of the medical staff from the college is with him. They wanted to be sure we're here, because they're sending him home in an ambulance."

CHAPTER THREE

Margaret met them at the door. An attendant pushed Professor Fontaine in a wheelchair, following Margaret into the living room. The attendant stopped at the sofa when Jacques put his hand up. "Right here is fine," he said.

Paul leaned forward awkwardly in one of the fireside chairs. His brow furrowed with concern.

Jacques stood from the wheelchair, insisting on settling on the sofa without help. But, always the gentleman, he dismissed the medic politely. "Thank you for your help, young man, but I'm really in good hands here, and if I need anything, I'll call my friend, Doctor Halliday."

The attendant spun the chair around. "Yes, sir." He nodded to Jacques.

Jacques Fontaine was a much-loved professor, chairman of his department, and well known in the community. A quarter of a century teaching at the university had ordered and disciplined his life. Instead of being daunted by the shadow of a stroke he suffered two years ago, his manner and routines had changed a little, but not his pride or his quiet strength. In some ways he was a softer, gentler man.

Always proud of Maddy and Paul, he had been at odds with his son from time to time, but since the shooting at the gallery, the friction was tempered with understanding.

"Time and a weakened heart may have altered my ability to cope with stress, but it hasn't lessened my will." He stretched a

21

hand toward Margaret. "If you wouldn't mind, Margaret, I could use a little scotch from the decanter on the sideboard."

"Didn't they give you something that might have adverse effects from alcohol, Pa?"

"No. Doctor Welch, from the med school happened to be in the building, but he had nothing with him when I blacked out. By the time the medics arrived, I was fully awake, and I refused to take anything. It was just a sudden dizziness and the shock of seeing the young man's body that made me lose consciousness."

Paul shook his head. "But you can't be sure of that, Pa. Why not let me call Doc Halliday?"

"I'll follow up with him tomorrow. Right now, all I can think about is that student and what could have possibly caused his death."

Margaret handed him the scotch.

"Did the police come?" Paul asked.

"Yes, but Doc Welch answered most of their questions because I was still dazed when they arrived. You have to understand that this all happened just two hours ago, just as I arrived at my office. I'm trying to remember the sequence, but what is most clear is that the dean was called in, and they were arranging to have the body removed and notify next of kin. By that time, an ambulance was there to take me home."

"Then you don't really know the cause of the student's death?"

"No, but there were no wounds on the body, no blood, and Welch thought it could be drug related. I know that the young man is—*was* in my Constitutional History course. He had an appointment with me for one-thirty. I don't have any files here to learn any more about him."

Jacques finished his drink and lay back on the sofa. "If he was a political-science major, I would remember more, but he wasn't. Doc thought he was first-year med, and probably took my course as an elective."

Jacques rubbed his fingers across his forehead. "The student didn't stand out in any way that I recall. More than that, I can't say without looking at the records."

"How about your computer files, Pa? Could I help find something for you on the laptop?"

Jacques slowly shook his head.

Margaret had been sitting on the edge of the fireside chair opposite Paul, listening. She suddenly stood. "I think I know what is needed here now, *mes amis*. Your papa should have a little quiet time, and I need your help, Jacques Paul. Come with me to the kitchen, okay?"

Paul moved away from Jacques and managed to follow Margaret's pace pretty steadily with his cane.

"Thank you, Margaret," Jacques called to her as they exited the living room.

"Now, Jacques Paul," she said, making their way down the hall to the kitchen. She put her finger to her lips and whispered, "I want you to call your sister right away and ask her to come here. Your papa needs moral support more than he does questioning, and Madelaine has a special way with him, eh?"

"What? I made him uncomfortable? You think I asked too many questions?"

"No more than the police probably did. Your papa is a very proud man. A very intelligent, proud man, and he needs to think this through on his own."

Margaret turned to face Paul as they came to the study door. "Let me tell you something, *mon chéri*. I was told at the retreat center about a famous person. His name escapes me right now, but what Sister Agatha quoted him as saying is very fitting to your papa's situation. He said 'God whispers to us in our pleasures, speaks to our conscience, but shouts in our pain.'

23

Your papa will hear Him. *Je suis sr.* Now go to his desk and make that call while I put tea on."

Paul limped into the study, his brow creased in thought. *She is a pistol! Comes up with one-liners that are jaw-droppers!* He covered his mouth with one hand and stared at the phone. *Je suis sr. I am sure, she says, like she's on a direct line to heaven. Maybe she is.*

He dialed the Donovans' number. Voice mail was on, so he reached in his pocket for his cell phone, checking for Maddy's cell number. His sister answered on the first ring.

"Paul?" she said. "What's going on? You hardly ever call my cell phone. Is there a problem?"

"Kind of, yeah. Where are you?"

"We're having dinner at Mia's with CeCe and Remi."

"Could you cut it a little short and come out to the Pool as soon as you finish? Pa has a problem and *Tante* Margaret thinks your presence would be a big help."

"What do you mean, he has a problem?"

"A death was discovered at the university and it hit Pa pretty badly."

"A death! Was it anyone we know?"

"No. It was a student."

"Is Papa okay?"

"Well, he passed out when the body was discovered." Paul heard Maddy draw her breath in deeply and let it out with a soft moan.

He could visualize startled faces reacting to Maddy. "Pa's insisting he's okay now, but as long as CeCe and Remi are with you, bring them along, babe. I could use their moral support, myself. Margaret thinks Pa needs you, and you know Auntie Mame. She leaves no doubt that she's in control."

When they arrived, *Tante* quickly followed Maddy into the living room with a tea tray. Paul sat at the kitchen table with Patrick, Remi and Clare. He repeated the scanty information that Jacques had given.

"Geez, Paul, your plate is full as it is," CeCe said. "Even though I think *Tante* will probably ease the situation for your dad, things couldn't get much tougher here for you."

"Yeah, they could, if Pa tells Kathleen what's happened, and she comes back."

Clare rolled her eyes and gave Paul a reassuring nod. "Gotcha. Not to worry, though. I'm sure Maddy will put your dad's mind at ease and encourage him to let us help if he needs it." Tilting her head toward Patrick, she raised her eyebrows and shot him a meaningful look.

Patrick nodded. "Anything he needs, Maddy or I could be out here in minutes."

Clare grasped Remi's arm. "I know it's not Marine Patrol business, but if the police get involved at the university, maybe you could get a pulse on what's happening."

After a long pause, Remi's glance went straight to Paul, then back to Clare. "I have a few connections that might shed some light on what happened at the university, but personally, I think Professor Fontaine can handle his end of it. It's his health that should be the primary concern here."

"You're right, Remi," Paul said. "Since his stroke, my father doesn't handle stress well, and I've burdened him with more than he deserves this month." He looked at each person in turn. "But that might just come to an end very shortly."

"What does that mean?" Clare asked.

Tante Margaret's sudden entrance into the kitchen saved Paul from answering. Her warm smile was calming. "Okay, everyone, I know you cut your dinner short to come here, eh, so I want you to have some dessert with Jacques Paul and me. My apple pie, baked just this morning."

Margaret kissed her daughter's cheek, erasing the frown on Clare's face. "*Ma Chéri,* you can please cut the pie." Margaret placed a reassuring hand on Paul's shoulder. "Your papa needed tea to calm him, but I think everyone else could take a little Irish coffee with my pie. What do you think, Patrick? Will you help me fix it?"

CHAPTER FOUR

CeCe and Remi left shortly after *Tante* persuaded Jacques to retire for the evening. "Catch you later, guys," Clare called from the door. Remi silently waved.

"Nothing can be solved tonight anyway," Maddy assured her dad. "We'll be right behind you if you need us tomorrow, or whenever. We're just a phone call away, Papa."

Patrick and Paul joined Maddy in the living room after *Tante* shooed them out of the kitchen. "Remi didn't have much to say tonight," Paul said. "He seemed a little distracted. Anything goin' on I don't know about?"

Lifting his shoulders in a shrug, Patrick looked at Maddy. "I think Remi's getting tired of waiting for CeCe to set a wedding date," he said.

"That may be, but there's more to it than that," Maddy said. "True, it's been almost a year since they got engaged, but ever since Remi's dad was diagnosed with lung cancer Remi's been spending most of his spare time at the inn. He either takes his dad to radiation or spells his mother so she can take him. CeCe hardly sees him more than once or twice a week. When she's on the day shift, Remi's working, and when she's on nights, he's at the inn trying to help."

"God, I've been out of the loop so long I didn't even remember about Remi's dad. The prognosis isn't good?"

"Not so far. Even *Tante* Margaret has been over there helping Mary Windspirit at the B and B."

"Sounds like something *Tante* would do. When Pa told me he was going to ask her to come here, he said something that was pretty profound, considering he's married to Kathleen. Pa said, 'If anyone could sustain my life other than God, it would be Margaret.' " Paul nodded with a smile. "She sure has the pulse of things here. Not to worry though, sis. As soon as we get some answers, I'll call you, okay?"

Paul put his laptop aside and gripped the arms of the leather lounge chair in his room. He should be getting ready for bed. Instead, he stretched out one leg on the ottoman and sank back in the chair. He was setting his mind to do something he didn't want to do, but would do it anyway.

Suzanne Petrone. After his opening show at the gallery, Suzanne came up from New York, determined to be part of his life. So she said. No one knew she was in Maine, and Paul was happy to keep it that way for a while. *Got to be sure if I'm really the one and only.* Sizzling memories seared his mind . . . nights spent in a Portland hotel with Suzanne. He knew her body, but very little about her life. She traveled the globe as an art collector, but more than that he could only guess at.

The only niggling piece of information she'd inadvertently shared turned out to be as revealing as a mirror. The last time she was with him in New York, Suzanne told him she dropped the ending of her name. Petronelli sounded too Italian, too provincial for her taste. She changed it to Petrone.

Weeks later, the headlines hit. Well-known art dealer, Anthony Petronelli, imprisoned for selling forged copies of real masterworks. An FBI investigation brought him in with a few of his underlings. Tony Petronelli was an east-coast kingpin of an international syndicate. He was Suzanne's father. Paul read all the newspaper clips and followed the Internet postings about Petronelli's trial.

If he was honest with himself, he would admit that Suzanne *could* have been in on the gallery heist. She could have worked for her father. Naturally, she wouldn't talk about it, but the connection was a possibility and it festered like a sliver under the skin.

Suzanne left for Florida two days before the robbery, *for a little hiatus of fun and sun,* she said. Unbelievable that she would be going to the same town on the Gulf Coast where an art dealer was approached with a painting of *Les bateaux rouges Argenteuil.*

If she was there, in the town where the painting showed up, he would find her. The notion of her involvement with the theft was too easily believable to discard, and he had to know the truth. All of it.

Jacques's friend, Doctor Halliday had gone with him to check records and speak with the ill-fated student's professors at the medical college. As a distinguished alumnus, Bill Halliday had good connections at the medical school. He learned from a colleague, tipped off by a concerned roommate, that the student had recently been questioned about misuse of prescription drugs. That revelation seemed but a step away from a suspected overdose.

Jacques was told that the student's parents confirmed their son's depression over low grades at the end of his premed first semester. A logical next move was the appointment he made with Jacques to inquire about a program change. As department chair, Professor Fontaine would assess and advise, but that was the limit of his connection to the case.

A first death for the university, but the cause of death would remain a concern of the investigators. However, Jacques's reaction to the dead body became Doc Halliday's concern. Clearing him from any involvement in the death was the easy part of the day. Convincing him to have a CAT scan was the hard part.

"I really don't think it's necessary, Bill," Jacques said.

"I know you don't, but I'd be a poor physician if I didn't order it. I'll have the girl in my office set you up for tomorrow morning at the center, and she'll give you a call on the time later today."

Jacques Fontaine was resilient and reserved in a New England sort of way, but an underlying sadness showed about him when he returned home from meeting with Doc Halliday.

Margaret sensed it when he came into the kitchen.

"There was no room for wiggling with Doc Halliday," Jacques explained. "He took my blood pressure and scheduled a test for tomorrow morning."

"*C'est bon, mon ami.* A test is a good thing. You wouldn't want to collapse in front of your class and leave everyone wondering what's wrong with Professor Fontaine."

Jacques smiled at her logic. "Of course not, but what happened to me yesterday was very unusual. I know Doc is trying to rule out possible causes, but honestly, Margaret, I'm not worried about myself. It's Paul I'm worrying about. Just when I should be helping him, I may be the one needing help."

"Worry is a hard pillow, but I am here to soften it for you, *chèri.* Paul is in the study. He's been waiting for you, and I think he has something to tell you. Go to him and I'll bring tea in."

"I'll do that, but bring the pot of tea for you and Paul. I'm going to have my scotch. It's my one a day, Margaret." He grinned as he left the kitchen with a lighter step than when he entered.

"Hey, Pa, you're looking better. Did you have good news?"

"No. Death rarely holds good news, Paul. No firm conclusion about the student's death until the autopsy, but a lot of circumstances that clear me and my department from suspicion."

30

"You must be relieved about that, huh?"

Jacques nodded. "Yes. Evidence of prescription-drug addiction is suspected."

"Geez. Death from drugs! That'd be a bad rap for the university, wouldn't it?"

"It may be a first here in my tenure, but it's certainly not so across the nation. One small caveat is the young man's friends who spoke highly of him and worried about him. I'm hoping that an unknown medical problem will surface in the autopsy. People turn to drugs for all kinds of reasons. That could change the picture."

"Talk about medical problems, what did Doc Halliday say about you?"

Jacques sipped his scotch, his gaze lingering on Paul before answering. He sat back against the pillows on the window seat. "Oh, Doc's just being cautious. He ordered an ultrasound for tomorrow. Ruling out causes for the fainting, you see. Told me my physical activity was too limited during this past winter. I need to walk more, avoid stress, and lose some weight. Hopefully, the tests will show there's nothing to be concerned about. That's what I told Margaret when I came through the kitchen."

"Fat chance of losing weight with Margaret *in* the kitchen."

"She said you have something to tell me, Paul."

"Yeah, actually she put a bee in my bonnet. Margaret told me things about Sean Michael Rafferty that convinced me what I have to do."

"Rafferty? I'm afraid I'm not following."

"Mr. Rafferty, the philanthropist, the man behind Cornerstone Gallery. The guy you told me was funding all kinds of things in town."

Jacques's fingers flew to his forehead. "Yes, of course. I remember now. It took a minute for the name to register."

"Margaret painted him as a really understanding guy. She

gave me the incentive to telephone him."

Jacques's eyebrows danced up, and he leaped to his feet at the sight of Margaret coming through the door with a tea tray.

"What's this? Did I hear my name?" she asked, looking suspiciously at Paul as she placed the tea tray on the desk.

"Yes, but only good stuff about you, *Tante*. I was telling Pa about the call I made to Mr. Rafferty. The man was very understanding."

"Given that you've been incapacitated ever since the break-in, I don't see how he could be anything less than understanding," Jacques said. "The police investigators documented everything and cleared you. You were shot during the robbery, for God's sake."

"We talked about the stolen painting showing up in Florida, and I asked his counsel about my going there to have a look-see for myself. Surprisingly, Mr. Rafferty liked the idea, but he has to check first with a private investigator who's working for him."

Tante Margaret's demeanor changed immediately. *"Voicee!"* she said, with a knowing smile. "I have a premonition sometimes about people, you know. I get feelings about things that may happen. I think Sean Michael Rafferty is going to help you, Jacques Paul."

Paul shot a glance at his father, and shook his head. "I dunno. I wish I could be as sure as you, Auntie Mame."

"Pray to the good Lord, *mon cherie*, and He will steady your heart and help you move forward with this."

Margaret handed him a cup of tea. Paul looked at the face that smiled at him with such compelling eyes. He smiled back and let his smile serve as a pause while he searched for words.

CHAPTER FIVE

Margaret insisted on dragging a canvas folding chair across the dunes before the first streaks of light hit the sky. Paul was all set up by seven A.M., a thermos of coffee, sketch pad and pencils in a picnic basket perched in the sand at his side.

Tante is quick to give her opinion, but a softie when you'd never expect her to be. Who else would be up before dawn, ready to help me set up?

Spring cool air breathed in with the tide. Paul rubbed his hands together and grabbed his sketch pad. The sun had barely crested the horizon. Instead of birds streaking their way through ribbons of orange and amber light, the *Argenteuil, Red Boats* filled his vision. Every time he looked to the horizon, Monet's sailboats suffused his gaze.

Claude Monet, the most lyrical of the impressionists, was one of Paul's favorite artists. Suzanne knew that. He couldn't believe his eyes when she showed up with the oil painting.

"A little acquisition from the Museum of l'Orangerie at the Tuileries, during my last trip to Paris," she'd said with a sly smile. "The *Les bateaux rouges Argenteuil* is from a private collection. The collector is one of my best contacts."

Paul was well aware that the Paris museum closed in 2000 for renovation. He read about the removal of works after a grand exhibit of paintings; some from other museums, some from private collections. There was no reason then to doubt her word.

"No big deal, my love," Suzanne had said. "I have carte blanche as to where I could place it for exhibit." God knows what she *did* to wangle that deal from its owner.

He tried to focus on the cadence of the sea, but her face appeared and reappeared with the cresting waves. "Enough!" Paul finally shouted. He shook his head and shoulders as though to shake her out of his mind. *I promised to sketch. . . .* Musical notes from his cell phone skewed his first pencil stroke. "Who in hell is calling at this hour?" Paul said aloud, pulling his phone out of his jeans. He smiled at the readout. "Who else! Hey, CeCe, what's up?"

"Sorry to call so early, but I just got off night shift and wanted to catch you before *Tante*'s ears were around."

"Her ears were around at dawn, babe. Your *tante* is one helluva persuasive woman, but I guess you know that. I'm out on the beach, sketching the sunrise. Her idea, and she's going to come out after me in a while."

"Well, I'm glad she's got you up and out, because that's part of the reason for this call. Your sister suggested I come get you later on, and maybe you and I can meet up with Remi for a drink and then go over to their place for pizza."

"That sounds like a conspiracy. I thought you were calling to tell me you missed me and *Julie's Dream*, but, hey, I don't mind being the odd guy in two's company. What's the other part of the reason?"

"Oh, it's just me, wondering if *Tante* is really needed out there. You'd be the best person to know. I know your dad wants her at Francois's Fancy, but you know how my mom dives into things, always wanting to help—I'm afraid she'll get in over her head, and that could spell trouble with a capital T."

"I think I know what you're getting at, Cec, but listen to this. Margaret encouraged me to get more involved with the gallery-theft investigation, and her idea paid off. I called Cornerstone's owner at her suggestion, and the result was surprisingly good. So I'd have to say your fears are unfounded."

"Not for long, Paul. I'm warning you. This may just be the beginning. *Tante* immerses herself into things. Let me refresh your memory when we talk later. I need a little shut-eye first, so I'll pick you up at four, and we'll go to the Yardarm, okay?"

"I'll be ready."

Clare blurted out the issues she'd been dealing with as they drove down Mile Stretch Road. First, *Tante* Margaret leaving her house to stay at Francois's Fancy, the possibility of *Tante* becoming too involved with the gallery theft, and, most importantly, getting in harm's way. She reminded him about *Tante*'s head injury and the deaths that occurred after Margaret's psychic powers catapulted Remi's investigation into a full blown, FBI-involved drug bust.

Next she confided her worries over Papa Jacques's latest scare at the university, and last, but really first and foremost, her fiancé, Remi. "You guys think alike, Paul. No matter what the problem, bottom line is fathers and sons have strong ties. I remember when you flew home when Papa Jacques had the stroke. You two may have been at odds, but it was you who finally pulled him out of a slump at the hospital."

"I think I tend to remind Pa of what he lost . . . with Mom, you know . . . with my painting and all." Paul shrugged. "On the other hand, he has Kathleen now."

"Sort of like Jamie Windspirit and Mary, huh? Remi's blood mother died, but Mary's been as much a mother to Remi as *Tante* is a mom to me."

"Whoa! No way could Kathleen ever be a mother to me. She may be the apple of Pa's eye, but we're talkin' apples and oranges. Mary Windspirit is a wonderful woman, and I can see why Remi has put his life on hold for his dad right now. They both need him."

"I know, but I need him too, and I just don't seem to be part of his life lately."

"Geez, Cec. That can't be totally true. You were my two special people at the gallery opening."

"Yeah, but that was last year, just after the investigation got resolved. Remi promised to make time for me then, and he did. We both tried hard to juggle our schedules so we could be together. It was like my star was really working for me. We used to talk a lot about marriage, you know. Like, where we'd live, and what kind of house we wanted, and how many kids we'd have." Clare pulled into a parking spot in front of the Yardarm. She closed her eyes for a second. "And then his father was diagnosed with cancer."

"I wish I could quote one of *Tante*'s aphorisms. I'm at a loss here. What is it you think I could do or say to Remi that's going to help?"

"For starters, you guys think alike. Maybe you could talk to him about Jacques and how you feel about causing stress when your dad's health is so shaky. There is sort of a parallel, don't you think?"

"That's a stretch, Clare. He might open up to me if you weren't around, but—" Paul shook his head, threw his hands up and shot Clare a questioning smile. "Stranger things have happened over a few drinks. Maybe it'll be good just to change the atmosphere for him, and being with Patrick and Maddy might help."

"That's what your sister had in mind."

"Then call him and make it hard to refuse."

Clare dialed Remi's number before they got out of the car. His cell phone was on voice mail, so she left a message. "Hi, Remi. Paul, you, and I have been invited to the Donovans' for pizza. I think we all need a break, so come join Paul and me at the Yardarm and we'll go to Maddy's together. Five-thirty, okay?"

"That sounded positive, Cec. Let's go in and raise a glass and hope he shows."

Inside, the Yardarm was beginning to fill up for happy hour. They chose a booth near the door, and Paul brought a pitcher of beer from the bar.

"This is the first beer I've had in a month. The meds interfered with my preferred libations, and between Kathleen and now your *tante*, I've had enough tea to run competition with Boston harbor." Paul poured the amber brew and raised his glass. "*Slainte,* Cec. Remember the Gaelic?"

Clare's voice dropped to a sigh. "Yep. Every time I hear that toast, I think of new beginnings. That's what Maddy raised a toast for when Patrick proposed. I could use some new beginnings myself right about now."

"Me, too. Number one, I'd like to throw this damned cane away, and number two, I want the painting found and the gallery back to normal."

A sudden wail of sirens had heads turning at the bar. "Sounds pretty close," Paul said, craning his neck to the window to see if emergency vehicles turned the corner toward Mile Stretch Road. "I'm still nervous about Pa. He was taking a nap after his tests this morning. He sure as hell won't sleep through that siren if it goes up Mile Stretch Road."

"Doc Halliday won't have test results for a while, but it's good that Papa Jacques is resting. Did Doc give him orders?"

"Kind of. He actually second-guessed the situation yesterday. Doc thinks Pa may have had a TIA. I never heard of that, and *Tante* told me that TIAs are commonly known as mini strokes."

"Ayuh. She's right. Transient ischemic attack. They're caused by a clot blocking the blood supply to the brain, and tests like a carotid ultrasound or an MRA could prove it." Clare looked at

Paul's troubled face and placed her hand over his. "TIAs are sometimes a warning sign of things to come, but not always."

"Geez, Cece." Paul laced their fingers together. "This is not good."

A shadow suddenly loomed over their booth, and Paul looked up, jerking his hand away. "Hey, Remi. With all the noise in here, we didn't hear you come in."

Clare shoved over in the booth, but Remi stood there in his patrol uniform, not moving.

"Guess not," he said, staring stonily at Paul. "Got your message, Clare, but I only came in to tell you I can't make it to the Donovans'. I'm on a call down to the gut. Fishing-boat accident heading up to the basin. Catch you later," Remi said, turning away.

Paul jumped up and caught Remi's arm; walked with him to the door. "Things are not what they seem here. Clare was explaining a medical term about my father's condition, and I impulsively reached for her hand at the bad news. We were commiserating—your father, my father. Nothing more." Paul looked up into Remi's troubled eyes. "Clare's hurting, Sarge. She misses you."

Remi looked away for a second. "I know," he said with a catch in his voice. He gave Paul's shoulder a squeeze before he went out the door.

Back at the booth, Clare's eyes welled with tears. "Nothing works for me," she said, fumbling in her purse for a tissue.

Paul pulled a handkerchief out of his pocket, dabbed her cheeks with it, and folded it into her hand. "It's gonna be all right, Cec. I told him what we were talking about and why I grabbed your hand." He pushed Clare's chin up with one finger. "I told him you miss him. Okay?"

"As if that would make a difference."

Paul raised his shoulders in a shrug. "I think it did. Remi

said, 'I know.' Blow your nose, drink up and let's get out of here before somebody thinks I'm the one who made you cry."

CHAPTER SIX

Maddy stood back from the open door, gazing from Paul to Clare. "No Remi?"

"He's on a call. A fishing-boat accident near the basin," Paul said.

Maddy kissed her brother on the cheek and pulled Clare into a hug. "Come in the kitchen, CeCe. The pizza just arrived and Patrick's waiting in the family room. Go on in, Paul. He'll pour you a beer. We'll bring the pizza in a minute."

Maddy wrapped an arm around Clare's shoulder and cocked her head to look into her eyes. "*Tante* just called. She asked us to call her back as soon as you got here, so maybe you should do that first. Use the phone in here while I get the pizza out of the box."

"It's not like *Tante* to be checking up on me. Did she sound okay?"

"Well, yes, but I don't think it's about you. She said something about a phone call that came this morning, then she had to hang up quickly for some reason, and that's when she asked us to call her back. I didn't get much more than that, because she was whispering."

"*Tante* whispering?" Clare clicked on Fontaine's number from Maddy's directory. Margaret's voice sounded loud and clear this time.

"Sorry, *ma chéri*, I had to cut my call short the first time because Jacques was coming down the hall to the kitchen. I wanted to explain to you and Madelaine without Jacques's ears hearing. I need to hear what you think about the phone call, eh?"

"Mom, slow down and start over. I don't know what phone call you're talking about."

"Kathleen. She called this morning when Jacques was out having tests. I had to tell her because she knows it's Saturday and Jacques should be home. I tried to make it all sound like routine. 'He will tell you about it,' I told her. 'Everything is good here at Francois's Fancy,' I said. 'Jacques Paul's leg is much better.' I tried to ask about Kathleen's *tante,* you know, but Kathleen wanted to talk about Jacques!"

"Well, did you tell her about the student's death?"

"No, no! That's not for me to do. Jacques didn't call Kathleen about it last night because he was exhausted mentally and physically. I think he's going to call her tonight, though."

"I'm not sure what you are trying to tell us, *Tante.*"

"Listen to me, Clare Margaret. I know how Jacques Paul would react to Kathleen's call if he had answered the phone. I know how he feels about her, and he would not want her flying back here. For me, I'd just like some peace of mind about what I said, or didn't say, to Kathleen. God forbid if Jacques really needs her back here right away." Clare held the phone close to Maddy's ear so she could hear *Tante*'s words.

"I don't know what Jacques's tests will show," she continued, "so I don't know the danger he may be in. You know about these things. You are the nurse, *cherie.* And Madelaine is the daughter. Do you or Madelaine think I soft-pedaled things, too much, maybe? I am asking for your opinions, my darlings."

Clare spoke softly into the phone. "In other words you're feeling guilty because you didn't tell Kathleen the whole truth." Clare shot Maddy a questioning look as she rolled her eyes. Maddy nodded and mouthed, "It's okay," in a whisper.

"Well, Mom, if I had answered the phone, I probably would have done the same as you, and Maddy agrees with me. I might have thrown in a few medical terms to convince her not to worry, but you shouldn't give it any more thought. Just relax and let Jacques handle Kathleen. The wrinkles will iron out. That's what you always tell me."

"Damn." CeCe said when she hung up the phone. "Things couldn't get any more screwed up." She crowded close to Maddy's ear to whisper. "I don't think Paul needs to know about Kathleen's call, do you? It's just one more complication, and he has enough on his plate already."

Maddy nodded. "I agree. Let's get this pizza in to the family room."

Margaret lifted the dust cloth away from the mirror's gilt edge, studying her reflection. She turned a little sideways, scowling at the gray hairs threaded through the coronet of braids at the back of her neck. *"Mon Dieux,"* she muttered. "Time I did something about this." Up until last year Margaret had been totally comfortable with herself and her beloved, adopted daughter, Clare. She couldn't really pinpoint when things began to change.

Maybe it was after she realized that Clare was seriously in love with Sergeant Remi Windspirit. Clare had lived independently since she graduated college and started work at the medical center, so losing her to Remi shouldn't change their relationship that much. But lately it had.

Maybe it was the death of Maddy and Patrick's child. Clare's lifelong friendship with Maddy had led *Tante* Margaret in and out of Fontaine family woes since the girls were in kindergarten. The crib death of Julie Margaret affected all their lives.

Maybe it was Jacques. His latest debacle at the university coming on the tail of his son's gunshot wound seemed too much for Jacques to bear.

It could be none or all of the above. Her hair was turning gray, and she didn't like it.

She ran her dust cloth over the dining-room table, pausing to gaze out the window at the stretch of beach that glittered far to the southwestern edge of Fletcher's Neck. The rose-sparkled sand glistened in the morning sunlight. It was still too early for Jacques Paul to be down for breakfast. She heard him come in last night, his cane thudding on the stairway and his bedroom door opening and closing. *Tante* was staying in Maddy's old room, right next to Jacques Paul's bedroom.

If he didn't come down by nine, she would have to wake him. The professor had made known his wishes to go to ten-o'clock mass at Star of the Sea chapel.

"What's this? Cleaning on Sunday morning?" Jacques said as he entered the room.

Margaret smiled and shook her head. "Just a little dusting before I set the table. Sit down, Jacques, and I'll bring coffee and juice in. Madelaine sent Jacques Paul home last night with some of Mrs. Donovan's scones. I found them with a note in the kitchen. Should I bring them in for you this morning?"

"One will be just right for me with my coffee. Doc Halliday's orders are to watch my diet. Low fat, he says. Okay, Margaret?"

"*Oui,* I will try to remember." Margaret set three places at the table before hurrying back to the kitchen. Neither of them heard Paul coming down the stairs. He startled Jacques when he walked slowly into the dining room, trying to balance without leaning too heavily on his cane.

"Mornin', Pa. Looks like we're gonna have breakfast in here, huh."

"Yes. Margaret's idea. She says Sundays are special. It's a good surprise to find you up early and down here without help. How did you manage that?"

"The leg is doin' better, or maybe I've learned the rhythm of my cane. I made it down without a problem. It's amazing what that little jaunt with CeCe did for me. Last night was the first I've been out of here other than trips to the doctor, and I think it was good therapy."

Margaret came through the pantry carrying a large tray. "Good morning, Jacques Paul." She beamed a smile his way as she set the tray on the sideboard. "Your papa is having the scones Madelaine sent. What can I get for you, *mon chérie?* Would you like eggs?"

"Yes, that sounds good. Over easy is how I like them, but you don't need to wait on me, *Tante*. I used to be pretty good in the kitchen and I ought to get back into action."

Margaret patted Paul's shoulder where he stood next to the big oak buffet. "Help yourself to juice, Jacques Paul, and sit. I like to wait on you."

When Margaret returned with Paul's eggs it was very quiet in the dining room. She sat down, poured coffee and traded looks with father and son. "You two are mighty quiet on such a fine Sunday morning. Is your breakfast all right, Jacques Paul?"

"Mmmm," Paul said, continuing to eat without meeting her eyes.

"I've just shared the news I received from Kathleen," Jacques said.

Margaret drew in her breath. "Did you tell her about the student at the university?" she asked.

"Yes. I felt I needed to explain *why* when Kathleen said she called here yesterday and you mentioned I was out having some routine tests."

"*Oui,* Jacques. I'm sorry I forgot to tell you, but I tried not to alarm her. I explained where you were when she called, but that's all I told her. Was I wrong?"

"No, no. It's all right, Margaret. Kathleen is determined to stay on with her aunt, but only until I've heard from Doc Halliday. She's prepared to fly home if I need her."

Paul cleared his throat and pushed his chair back. "Breakfast was great, *Tante*. Thanks. I think I'll get a little air out back. I won't stray far, Pa. Whenever you're ready for church, give a holler or toot the horn." Paul was careful to make his pace look effortless as he went through the pantry to the back door.

"I'm amazed that Jacques Paul has made such improvement in the last two days. I'm so happy for him," Margaret said.

Jacques's expression seemed more puzzled than pleased. "I'm not so sure his improvement is genuine. I suspect Paul might be masking his discomfort purposely, so as not to worry me. What's really true is that Paul does not want to be here with Kathleen and me. The house holds too many memories of his mother."

"Ah, *mon ami,* that is sad, but true. Even I feel Julie's presence here in these rooms." The words were out before she could stop them. She covered her mouth with her fingers, feeling a flush creep up her neck. Her throat went dry, but she managed to keep an even expression. The hall clock chimed, breaking the silence.

"Please, one moment. I meant no offense about Kathleen. I feel so at ease with you, Jacques, that I say whatever is on my mind without thinking. You and I can still converse in the language we grew up with and we have many ties. My Clare and your Madelaine . . ." Margaret stood, placing her hand on Jacques's arm. She smiled at him. "And Jacques Paul. We have our faith, too, eh?"

Jacques nodded and smiled. "We are together in our faith, yes, Margaret."

"When my head was injured during Remi's investigation, you told me, 'Have faith and God will sort things out.' The good Lord did just that."

Margaret rose and began to clear the table. "Whatever I can

do to help, you know, I will do my best."

Jacques placed his napkin on the table. "I've no doubt of that, my dear." He picked up his plate and nodded toward the pantry. "Time to go to church, Margaret."

CHAPTER SEVEN

Clare parked next to Remi's truck in the parking lot behind King's Castle Inn. ~CLOSED~ The sign out front had her mind whirling. The windows were shuttered and the inn was dark. *When did this happen?* She had the feeling that it was not a typical Sunday morning closing.

Remi had given no hint that his father was worse, but then, Clare hadn't actually talked to him since last week. He did say there had been no guests, but the *Queen,* so called by Remi and his dad, "declares it's still mud season and she's not concerned."

Clare tucked the foil-wrapped zucchini bread under her arm and closed the car door. Glancing back at the rear of the inn, at the turrets and gables, then at the upstairs windows of Remi's garage apartment, she chided herself for her indecision. *Come on Clare. You spent half the night thinking about this. Just do it!* She climbed the stairs. Hesitating at Remi's door, she drew in her breath when it opened just as her hand reached to knock.

"Clare!" Remi, arms loaded with clothes and bed linen, stopped in the doorway. He motioned her inside with his head. "You surprised me, but if you'll come in and wait for a minute, I'll be right back. I'm just dropping laundry off at the house," he called over his shoulder as he went down the stairs. "For Mrs. Boudreau. She comes tomorrow."

Clare sat in the only chair in the room, Remi's desk chair. *Mrs. Boudreau is Mary Windspirit's hired help. Why is she coming if the inn is closed?* Clare stared at a map of North Carolina spread out on the desk. Her eyes roamed the room. An open duffle bag sat near the closet, and Remi's laptop was open on the bed at the far end of the room. She left her purse and bread on the desk and moved to the bed.

A Delta Airline itinerary for Jamie and Mary Windspirit was detailed on the screen of the open laptop. Puzzled by what she was reading, she didn't hear Remi come back until his arms came around her.

He whispered in her ear. "I intended to come tell you about this after I finished up at the inn."

She swirled around to face him. "Finished up? I don't understand. Are you going somewhere too? What about your dad?"

Remi drew her into his arms, pressing her head against his chest. "You feel so good in my arms, Clare. I've neglected you for much too long." He kissed her soundly, then tugged her to sit beside him on the bed.

"I'm not going anywhere, except to stay at the inn for a while. My dad is in remission, and my mom and dad have made some plans. When I got home from that duty call the other night, my folks told me they're taking a trip to see my half sister in North Carolina. They already had their reservations." Remi shook his head, pointing at the laptop. "I guess you saw that. My sister and her husband work for the National Park Service and haven't been able to get time off to come to Maine to see Dad, so my folks are going there."

"Is he really strong enough for that?"

"Strong or no, he wants to do it, and Mom is all for it. She says they should get away from responsibilities here for a while, and I agree. They've closed the inn, but I think that was a plan to give me a break, too. Mom thinks it will be easier if I stay at the inn so I can fix my meals and take care of any emergencies."

Remi grinned. "I told her I know a really good cook who might help."

He cradled her face in his hands and kissed her again, more urgently this time.

"We could be together here," he murmured, kissing the fingers of her left hand. He circled his finger around her engagement ring.

Clare drew back and met his gaze. Her eyes, that strange combination of gray and blue, were brimming with tears. "I was beginning to give up on that ever happening, Remi." She swallowed hard and squeezed his hand. "I came here today hoping for a woman-to-woman talk with your mom. I intended to ask her if she thinks you want to call off our engagement."

A muscle in his jaw twitched and Remi closed his eyes, silently shaking his head.

Clare didn't wait for an answer. "From what I've observed, I think Mary knows your heart better than you do, and I'm convinced she'd give me a straightforward answer."

"Yes, she would, but so would I if you asked. I can't believe you'd even think something like that."

Clare could see the hurt in his eyes.

Remi nodded, still holding tightly to her hand. "The Queen would have told you what she knows to be true. I love you beyond telling, Clare Chamberlaine."

"Oh, Remi," she managed, choking back her tears. "I needed to hear that. I should have had more faith in you. You told me once that faith and doubt often exist together."

"Nothing is going to separate us, Clare. I am like the wild swan. I will only give my heart once, and I gave it to you, freely, a long time ago," he said, gathering her into his arms.

Jacques didn't know what awakened him so early. The only sound came from outside. Breakers rolling in to shore at high tide. He rose slowly from the big four-poster and walked to the tall windows fronting the dunes. Streaks of red and gold of the rising sun rippled on waves crashing against the rock, and the wind was kicking up. "Hmm," he said aloud. "Strange time of year to have such a high tide, and red is not a sailor's delight."

He donned robe and slippers, walked with care down the stairs and through the hall to his study, determined to spend some quiet time before anyone was awake.

Pale yellow light drifted through the shutters of the guest room at Francois's Fancy. Margaret stretched and sat up to rest her back against the chintz-covered headboard. It was a pretty room, she thought: soft green walls adorned with white framed paintings of seashells. She was sure this used to be Maddy's bedroom. An old-fashioned maple ladies' chair, skirted and cushioned with the bed's matching chintz, stood under the windows next to a wicker table. A photo of Maddy and Clare was perched on the table. It looked like a pose from the nineties.

Her feet flew over the cold pine floor to a braided rug in front of the table and chair. She examined the photo carefully, convinced she was right about this bedroom. *The girls were so young. Clare strongly resembles her biological mother, not her papa. I see very little of my family in her face, except for her black hair.*

Margaret crossed the room and turned this way and that before a mirror above a maple dresser. *I do have my* grand-mère's *genes, le plus certainement,* she thought, pushing back the tousled ebony hair from her high, wide cheekbones. "I look like her, but I don't have to keep her style," she said aloud.

Reluctant as she was to use her inherited clairvoyant skills, Margaret could not deny her grandmother Henriette's half-French, half-Abenaki Indian heritage. As she continued to stare into the mirror, a strange thing happened, almost as though it was willed by Henriette. Margaret patted the coronet of braids at the nape of her neck and a phrase popped into her mind. She saw it flash across the mirror, just as it had been scrawled across a chalkboard in a long-ago Latin class. *Carpe Diem*—Sieze the day.

"Imagine that!" she spoke to the mirror.

Margaret dressed quickly and tiptoed down the hall, past closed bedroom doors and down the stairs, making her way through the dining room to the pantry, instead of through the long hall to the kitchen. She composed a mental list of the ingredients she needed for pancakes.

It was hard to be quiet in an unfamiliar kitchen. Drawers and cupboards had to be opened in a search for things. She had just finished chopping an apple into pancake batter when Jacques entered the kitchen.

"Margaret. I didn't realize anyone was up until I heard something out here. I mistook you for a field mouse rummaging through the kitchen. They do get in this time of year, you know."

Margaret laughed. "No wee creature, Jacques. Just big old me, trying to get breakfast started. I'm sorry if I woke you."

"Well, you didn't wake me, and you are not big, nor old. You're a delight to have around, Margaret. I've actually been up for a while, in the study correcting final-exam papers. I've put things on hold for the last few days, uh . . . well, you know why. I do need to catch up, though."

"*Oui*, I know." Margaret paused, wiping her hands on a towel. "Me, too," she said under her breath. "I've been thinking as I made this batter. I have something to do in town that may take a couple of hours, so if I have everything ready, do you suppose you and Jacques Paul could fix your own pancakes? He says he's at home in the kitchen, eh? So, would you mind this one time?"

"Of course not. Do whatever you need to do. We'll manage

fine. I'll take coffee into the study and wait for Paul to come down."

Jacques was content grading papers and sipping his coffee— for a while. He became restless when he heard Margaret leave the house. A concerned feeling tightened his gut and filled him with anxiety. When her car chugged out of the driveway he felt suddenly alone. *Nonsense. Paul is upstairs. It's these damned test results I'm waiting for that have me on edge.*

Distant thunder sent him to the window seat. Nothing could be seen through the window but a sudden great wash of rain. *Must have blown in right after I woke.* "Amazing that I didn't hear it," he said aloud as he turned back to the desk. His head jerked up in surprise.

Paul stood framed in the doorway, one hand resting on the study door. "If you're talking about the storm, it woke me out of a sound sleep. I barely got to the window before the rain came in, but I didn't bother checking on *Tante,* assuming she'd be down here early by habit. Have you had breakfast, Pa?"

"No, but Margaret made sure it was all prepared before she left. It's pancakes. I was waiting for you."

"She left? Where'd she go?"

"She said she had something to do in town this morning."

"Well, then, let's get started. It'll be good to get a hand in kitchen duty. I'll flip and you serve, okay?"

Threads of lightning danced across the study window. Jacques nodded toward the window as he left his desk. "Let's hope Margaret isn't caught somewhere in this storm."

"It's Clare who gets freaked out in thunderstorms, Pa. *Tante* should be okay. That old Chevy of hers is pretty reliable."

"I hope so," Jacques said, following Paul into the kitchen.

With the kitchen table set and everything at hand, fixing breakfast was an easy chore. Jacques poured juice and coffee and soon Paul brought a platter to the table, filled with stacks of apple pancakes.

"I don't have much of an appetite, but I'll try one," Jacques said.

Paul needed no urging to dig in. "These are so light, Pa, you're sure to want more. *Tante* Margaret is a wonder in the kitchen."

"Not just in the kitchen. Margaret is an all-around gem."

Rumbling thunder drowned out the sound of a car approaching. Minutes later, the kitchen door was thrust open with a bang, startling them out of their chairs.

"Sorry to barge in, but there's a helluva storm out there. Mile Stretch Road is a sheet of water." Doc Halliday stepped in, closed the door and hung his dripping hat on the doorknob.

Jacques was quick to take his coat. "Come sit down with us, Bill. I have an idea you didn't come for breakfast, but there's plenty here."

Paul took a mug from the cupboard and poured coffee. "Margaret made this coffee a while ago, so get ready for a jolt, Doc. Would you like a plate for pancakes?"

"No thanks, just hot coffee is what I need, Paul."

The house creaked and groaned as wind gusts whistled around the northwest corner of the kitchen, slashing rain against the kitchen window. Doc spoke without hesitation.

"My news is not good, Jacques, but it is hopeful. The tests showed that blockage in your left carotid artery is over eighty percent. The right is not so bad, but I'm recommending a cardiovascular surgeon take a look and give you a consult. He may want to do an endarterectomy. The risks are low, and that's the hopeful part. The surgery has lasting benefits and could help prevent future stroke or TIAs."

Paul watched his father pale. "What is an endarter . . . whatever you called it?" Paul asked.

"It's the most common treatment for carotid artery disease."

Bill faced Jacques. "The surgeon makes an incision in the neck and removes the plaque in the left artery, in this case. The artery is repaired with stitches or a graft. A couple of days in the hospital, and you'd be home again."

"Is there no other option?"

"There is angioplasty and stenting, but the long-term ability of it to *prevent* stroke is undetermined. I would prefer to wait and see for a while, Jacques. Watch out for dizziness or loss of balance, keep monitoring your blood pressure and continue with one aspirin a day." Doc pulled scripts from his pocket and laid them on the table. "I'm leaving you prescriptions. A blood thinner and medication to lower your cholesterol."

He pointed to the pancakes with a warning look, and shook his head. "Low-fat diet, Jacques. I do want you to consult with a cardiovascular surgeon to determine what's best, so I'm sending your records to Doctor Romano."

Jacques silently nodded his head.

"I know this is a lot to lay on you, buddy, but just so you don't forget, I do not routinely make house calls like this." He winked at Paul. "But I'm counting on you for a partner when the golf club opens."

Jacques's weak smile turned to fright when the back door suddenly flew open again. Margaret stumbled in, soaked to the skin, water puddling at her feet. Water trickled down her face like tears from hair that was plastered to her forehead. An incoherent sound escaped her lips when the men rose and moved toward her.

Jacques, first to her side, grasped her shoulders. "What happened, Margaret?"

Embarrassed past caution, Margaret laid her forehead instinctively on Jacques's chest for a second. When she looked up she spoke dejectedly. "My car stalled in deep water on Mile Stretch Road. Nobody came along, so I got out and walked."

Suddenly, her eyes widened, she spread the fingers of one hand across her mouth, and in seconds a determined, in-charge Margaret was back in control. She stepped back, shook her head, waving her hands wildly. "My umbrella blew inside out, and—" She stopped talking and covered the sides of her hair with her hands. *"Mon Dieu,"* she said, "it was supposed to be a surprise!"

Chapter Eight

Margaret stepped back from Jacques's arms. Her shoes made a sloshing, sucking sound at each step. She stooped to remove them, and a shuffling of feet nearby caught her attention. Standing near the table behind Paul, Doctor Bill Halliday had escaped her notice. She remembered the doctor, but this was no time for renewing an old acquaintance. *"Excuze moi,"* she said. Carrying her dripping shoes, she brushed past Paul and made a hasty exit from the kitchen.

"Judas Priest," Paul said. "I can't believe her car conked out."

"I can," Doc said. "The road already had inches of water when I drove up. That tells me I better trust my luck and try to get back to town, now, before it gets any worse." He clamped a hand on Jacques's shoulder. "I'll have the girls in the office make an appointment with Doctor Romano for a consult, Jacques. Call me for any reason, okay?"

Jacques nodded, attempting to smile. "I will. Thanks for coming out today, Bill. I didn't like the message, but I'm not going to hold it against the messenger."

When the door closed on Doctor Halliday, Paul whipped out his cell phone. "Who should I call about *Tante*'s car, Pa? Neither of us can get down the road in this weather, and there isn't much of a shoulder on Mile Stretch. We can't just leave it there."

"I think we'd best wait until Margaret comes downstairs. It's obvious she doesn't have a cell phone, or she would have called from the road, but she may have Triple A for all we know. I have things to do in the study, Paul. If Margaret needs help, call me."

Paul watched him leave the kitchen. Doc Halliday's recommendation was scary and Paul could tell from his father's expression that he was more than a little worried. *If Mom were here she would have the right words.* . . . Paul stared at the cell phone in his hand for an agonizing moment, then he laid it on the table.

After clearing the table and loading the dishwasher, he leaned one arm on the sink, pausing to ease his leg. Walking short distances without his cane was okay, but sustaining weight on the leg was not. He sat down at the table, head in one hand, and poured more coffee into his cup.

Thinking about *Tante* walking through the storm made Paul remember a past hurricane that had sent Maddy back in time. Details replayed in his mind. But this is not hurricane season yet and *Tante* isn't getting visions from the spirit world. She's here with us now, but what was she doing in town this morning? And what did she mean by the surprise?

He sipped his coffee, closed his eyes, picturing the gallery and willing images to come. Discreet advertising had brought art lovers, dealers and the curious to the gallery to see the Monet, but no images or suspicious scenes came to Paul's mind. When he opened his eyes, Margaret was coming through the pantry, taking soundless footsteps in her bedroom slippers.

Paul's eyes widened, heightening a look of surprise on his face. "Auntie Mame! You look so different. What happened?"

"What happened is I decided to join the twenty-first century." Margaret came to the table, patted her hair and did a little pirouette. "It's the first time my hair has been cut in many years, Jacques Paul. Clare's beauty shop did a nice job, but it got ruined in the rain. I did my best upstairs with the hair dryer, eh? What do you think, *cherie?*"

Paul stared at Margaret's short hair. Jet-black, shiny waves swept back on one side, and brushed forward on the opposite side with a bang. It framed her face with a soft, youthful look, a remarkable change.

"I think you look like a different person—a very beautiful one!"

Margaret's smile widened. "I wanted different. You like it, eh? Well, I was hoping to surprise you and your papa." Her smile transformed suddenly to a frown. "I know the doctor was here. Is Jacques somewhere with him?"

Paul pursed his lips and heaved a sigh. "No. Doc left and Pa is in the study. He's had some tough news, *Tante*. The tests showed blocked arteries and he may have to have some surgery down the road."

Margaret closed her eyes and whispered some French words that sounded like a prayer.

When her eyes opened, Paul reached for her hand. "Wait a bit before you talk to him about that, okay? I know he wants to take care of your car and that's a concern we both have." He picked up his cell phone from the table. "You didn't have one of these to call with, but do you have Triple A?"

"No. Clare wanted to give me a cell phone and the car plan for Christmas, but I refused."

"Well, if you want to be a twenty-first-century woman, then you have to have both." Paul stood, taking Margaret by the hand. "Come, my new lady, let's go see what Pa has to say."

Jacques was equally impressed with Margaret's new look. He puzzled, though, over the reason that she gave for her new hair style. *To keep up with the times?* Jacques always thought Margaret was comfortable in her own skin.

"Lovely, Margaret. It's just lovely," Jacques said.

"I told her she has to have a cell phone to be on track with everyone, Pa. She doesn't have Triple A, so what do you think we should do about her car?"

"I've given it some thought, and I think I'll call Patrick. The rain is letting up a little, and his truck shouldn't have a problem getting through the flooding. I'm sure he would come and tow your car the short distance to our drive, Margaret."

"Good idea, Pa."

"Then I'll make a nice hot lunch for everyone, okay?" Margaret asked. "I know Patrick takes bag lunches to his shop, so I think he would appreciate a hot meal."

"Uh, *Tante*," Paul said. "One of the things Doc said was that Pa should be on a low-fat diet. He has to be careful with calories, you know what I mean?"

"*Oui.* I'll talk to Clare tonight about this diet, but Jacques, what else did the doctor say?"

"The tests showed I have clogged arteries, Margaret. I have prescriptions to take and Doc wants to monitor my condition for a while. In the meantime, I'm to get a second opinion from a surgeon."

A frown creased Margaret's forehead. Jacques could tell she was disturbed, but he really didn't want to talk about surgery. "It's good that the college semester is ending," he said. "I'll have no trouble following a quieter routine; get a little exercise walking the beach, and catch up with my reading." He traded looks with Paul.

"I am uneasy about leaving your car there any longer, Margaret. We need to call Patrick. All right with you?"

His question hung in the air until Margaret nodded. She left the study as quietly as she had come in.

CHAPTER NINE

Pa was right, Paul thought. As Jacques had predicted, Patrick was quick to help. He towed Margaret's car to Francois's Fancy and was happy to stay for lunch. True to her word, Margaret made a hearty vegetable soup for lunch. She announced that she phoned Clare, asking for a copy of a low-fat diet from the dietary department at the medical center. Without a doubt, *Tante* gave CeCe the scoop about Jacques's tests, and Maddy would hear the details from Patrick. Before the day ended, everyone would know. Everyone but Kathleen.

Paul doubted that his father would tell her—not this soon—but when a phone call came after lunch, he wanted to be sure it wasn't Kathleen. He walked from the kitchen through the hall with the portable phone, but it wasn't Kathleen on the line. Sean Rafferty was calling from Boston. The pressure and tension, which had built up since Jacques's fainting episode, suddenly became a strange new mix of incredulous anxiety and relief that threw Paul into the eye of the storm.

Rafferty had arranged for him to meet next weekend with a special investigator working the case in Sarasota, Florida—all expenses paid, Rafferty said. Could he manage? Paul gave a lame excuse that he'd know right after he saw his doctor on Wednesday.

He stared at his leg, stretched out on an old chest that he dragged over to the porch rocker he sat on. His eyes lifted to the sea, sun-sparkled with thousands of diamonds rippling on crests of blue. There had been a magnificent rainbow after the storm, but it wasn't working any magic on Paul.

Voices quarreled in his head. One voice was relentless. *I accepted the* Les bateaux rouges Argenteuil *with too little investigation. My gut feeling is Suzanne may be tied up in this somehow. If I implicate her, our relationship goes down the tube and I also jeopardize my position at the gallery.* All the frustration he felt toward Suzanne came spewing out. He picked up his cane and struck at the floor with a resounding crack.

"I can barely make it through the dunes to the shore with this stupid thing. How the hell can I make it to Florida?"

Something Jacques said about *Tante* Margaret popped into his head. *If anyone could sustain my life, other than God, it would be Margaret.* No doubt about it, *Tante* is an "in charge" person, always ready to help, but could she help him now?

As though she was being summoned, Margaret pushed open the screen door and stepped out to the porch. She wrapped her arms inside a sweater thrown over her shoulders. "The air is cool out here after the storm, eh? Aren't the chairs all wet?"

Paul held up a ragged old beach towel. "I took care of that before I sat down. We keep these in this old sea chest," he pointed under his leg. "Come join me, *Tante*. You just missed the rainbow."

"A rainbow? My Clare would ask you if you made a wish." Margaret took the towel and gave a rocking chair another swipe before she sat down. She spread the towel over the porch railing to dry.

"Yeah, CeCe would have asked that. I remember her notions about astrology. She's a Sagittarian, right?"

"*Oui.* Clare learned all about the stars from my Jean, God rest his soul."

Paul looked at the face that smiled so serenely at him. *It was now or never.* "But you don't rely on astrology, Auntie Mame.

61

You have a better source. I remember how you tapped into your grandmother's energy during Remi's investigation. That was a powerful clue you gave him."

Margaret felt a blush rising in her face. "I can't deny that I have my *grandmère's* genes, but it's God who wraps us in a mantle of justice. That's what the good book says."

"I'm having a bit of trouble with God's justice right now."

"Trouble with God? I don't understand, *cheri.*" Margaret eyed the phone that sat on the table between their chairs. She waggled a finger at the phone. "Does it have something to do with a phone call you took out here?"

A sparkle of light flared in Margaret's eyes, forcing Paul to turn from her gaze. He had tried to steer the conversation toward Margaret's psychic ability, but she apparently didn't want to go there. *What now? Should I tell her about my suspicions? Could I trust her to find some element that would make sense of what really happened with Suzanne and the painting?*

The muscle in his cheek twitched. He nodded and drew a deep breath. "Yes. It was a phone call from Sean Rafferty. It's time for me to toe the mark, *Tante,* but unfortunately I'm not ready for the race."

She fixed him with her dark eyes as though she knew what he was trying to say. Then her eyes and her smile went soft and gentle. "Talk to me, Jacques Paul," she said.

It seemed Paul had a bottomless pit into which he poured everything he felt guilty about, starting with Sean Rafferty's call and his own hesitation to give him an immediate answer. He told Margaret about Suzanne, not his slip-sliding feelings for her and not the sex, of course, but about the *Argenteuil Bateaux Rouge* and its acquisition, and his need to find Suzanne and determine the truth. And finally, he told about the guilt he carried for leaving Jacques when his health is so precarious. "Geez, *Tante,* can you think of a worse mess to be in?"

Pity stirred inside her for Paul, but it wouldn't do to show it. For a long moment she stared at him.

"It is not such a mess, *cherie*. You just have to put things in proper order, eh? If the painting is first, then you must work step-by-step with the investigator. Your Ms. Suzanne . . . uh . . . maybe she is next. Does the special investigator know about her? You didn't mention her last name." Margaret shrugged. "But the police must have it, no?"

Paul shot a surprised look at Margaret. "*Tante!* I haven't told anyone about her except you." He shook his head, disgusted that he hadn't ever thought of Suzanne being investigated by the cops. "Apparently I haven't connected all the dots." *Jesus. Why did I think Suzanne exists exclusively in my own little world? An idiot could have made a connection between Petrone and Petronelli. She's probably already under investigation. That may be why Rafferty wants me down there.*

They sat quietly for a moment, the murmur of the sea and the creak of *Tante's* rocker making a steady rhythm, until Paul grasped Margaret's arm rest to stop her rocking. "Wait a minute. The little I know about investigative procedures came from Remi, last year when Clare and I discovered the dead body in the bay."

Tante winced.

"Who would have thought that scenario would turn into an FBI drug bust?"

"I don't like to remember that terrible time, Jacques Paul. The only good thing that came out of it is Remi Windspirit."

"Exactly, *Tante*. Remi! He may be just the guy to advise me about the best approach with this Florida PI. In the meantime, *Tante*, will you promise me you won't say anything to anybody about Suzanne?"

Margaret finished filleting a fresh fish that Paul brought home from the fish market. "I am going to bake some haddock for supper, if that sounds okay, Jacques. What would you like with it?" she asked.

"It's the *with-its* that I need to be careful of, but fish sounds good. I really don't want you to fuss, Margaret. I'll just have to get used to fewer desserts and less take-out food. Kathleen liked 'takeout or eat out,' you know." Jacques chuckled as though he was sharing a private joke about Kathleen, but actually, he was mentally comparing the two women, and Margaret scored tops in his kitchen, hands down.

Margaret grinned. "*Oui,* I know. None of that food for a while. I'm expecting Clare to stop by and bring me some guidelines from the medical center dietician. Then I'll feel better about putting the right food on your table."

"Is Clare working days this week?"

Margaret looked at her watch. "*Trois o'horlage! Aye yi yi.* She'll be here soon, Jacques," she said, hurriedly putting the fish under cover in the refrigerator. As she reached to untie her apron she took a whiff of her hands. "Phew, fish, eh? I must go upstairs and refresh a little. Clare hasn't seen me in a while and I want to look my best."

Paul and Margaret passed each other in the hall. Paul was walking slowly without his cane. "Jacques Paul, do you know if Remi is coming with Clare?" Margaret asked.

"Ayuh. I checked with him this morning and he said he would pick CeCe up and come out here with her right after her shift. The driveway is pretty full with your car and Pa's, so I was about to watch for them through the kitchen window." He placed a hand on her shoulder to stop her from hurrying to the stairs.

"Incidentally, *Tante,* when I drove to the fish market, I picked up a little something for you at the mall." He pulled the item from his pocket and put it into her hand. "It's all programmed and ready to go, but I'll explain it to you later, okay?"

Margaret's eyes widened. "A cell phone! *Mon Dieu.* You shouldn't do this, Jacques Paul. I don't know if I'm ready for these things."

Paul turned on his heel to start down the hall. "You are ready, Auntie Mame," he called over his shoulder. "Remember you are a twenty-first-century woman now."

When Paul got to the kitchen, Jacques was there, opening the door to Clare and Remi. "Come in, come in," Jacques said, kissing Clare's cheek and shaking Remi's hand. "I'm afraid I was indisposed when you were here last. It's good to see you, today."

Paul walked slowly forward, grinning. "Hey, guys."

"Geez, Cap, no cane?" CeCe asked. "Don't tell me my mom's working miracles outside the kitchen? Where is she, anyway?"

Paul laughed. "She may be at that, but I've been concentrating on getting around without a cane. *Tante* will be right down. She's upstairs cleaning up a bit."

Clare laid papers on the kitchen table. "*Tante* says she needs this diet information for you, Papa Jacques. How are you feeling?"

"Your *tante* probably told you about my test results. I'll be fine, Clare. I just have to be careful for a while and take my new meds." He smiled at Clare and turned away rather quickly, motioning to Paul with his hand. "Come, Paul, let's everyone go into the living room and wait for Margaret to come downstairs."

It was obvious that Jacques didn't want to talk about his health, and as soon as they settled into chairs, Paul attempted to change the subject. "No uniform today, Remi?"

"Nope, I'm taking a couple days off to do some things at the inn. My parents are away, and I'm kind of taking over for them."

"I hope that means your father is better, Remi?" Jacques asked.

Before Remi could answer, Clare suddenly shot out of her chair, shouting, "Mom!" Heads swiveled to the entry as Margaret breezed into the living room. She was wearing a pretty sweater and skirt that Clare had never seen, but it wasn't the clothes that startled Clare. "OhmiGod, Mom. What did you do?"

Margaret strolled in like a model on a runway. She stopped at the ottoman in front of Jacques's wing chair and sat as regally as a queen. "It's my new haircut," she said, patting her hair. "Don't you like it, *cherie?*"

Clare came forward, slack jawed, tilting her head and leaning over Margaret to view the back of her hair. "I can't believe it. Who did this?"

"Sally's Cut-n-Curl, where you go, eh? Sally told me I had a natural wave which worked nicely into this style."

"I can see that, but why? For as long as I can remember you've always had a neat, braided bun in the back."

"Hey, Cec," Paul said, "times change. Cut your mom some slack. How about: 'Gee, you look great,' or 'What a nice change.' "

Clare's serious look faded to a smile. She stood back, hands on hips and nodded. "Paul's right. Your hair does look great, Mom, but still . . . am I missing something?"

Margaret stood and mimicked Clare's hands-on-hips posture. "Okay, my darling. My turn. Did you bring the diet information?"

"Yes. I left it on the kitchen table."

"Then let's go to the kitchen." Margaret took Clare's arm, propelling her. "You can help me plan some menus and maybe you'll find out if anything's missing."

Remi shook his head, laughing as he watched them leave. "I

have to admire Margaret. She reminds me of my mom."

"Margaret *is* much to be admired, Remi," Jacques said, "but when she made her entrance, you didn't have a chance to tell me about your dad. You said your parents are away?"

"Yes. They flew to North Carolina to visit my sister. My dad is in remission. He insisted he felt strong enough to take the trip and my mom agreed they should. So . . ." Remi shrugged.

Jacques nodded. "It's wise to follow one's convictions. I hope they have a good trip."

"Did they leave you in charge of the inn?" Paul asked.

"Not really in charge, no. The inn is closed, but I am going to be staying there—doing a little work around the place and, you know, making sure everything's running okay, things my dad did routinely."

"They are fortunate to have you, Remi," Jacques said.

Paul shifted uncomfortably in his chair. "I wish I could do that kind of thing around here, but"—he gestured openhandedly—"suddenly, things have changed."

"Everyone understands your position, son. You've made good progress, especially this week, Paul."

"No, Pa. I'm not talking about my leg or my job. I mean there really is a change in the works, *today*. I haven't had a chance to tell you, but do you remember *Tante*'s premonition about Sean Rafferty helping me?"

Jacques nodded.

"Well, *Tante*'s prediction happened. I got a phone call this morning from Mr. Rafferty. He offered to send me to Florida."

CHAPTER TEN

Remi frowned. "Do you mind if I ask who Rafferty is?" he asked.

"Sean Rafferty is a wealthy philanthropist who put up the money to start Cornerstone Gallery," Paul answered.

Jacques pushed forward in his chair, surprise and interest mingled on his face. "If you are to meet with Rafferty's investigator, did he say when this would happen?"

Paul took a deep breath. "Yeah, he did, Pa. He's talking about next weekend, but I told him I had to get my doctor's okay first." Paul turned his gaze to Remi. "I was really stalling, you know. I don't want to walk into this, cold turkey. I was hoping maybe you could tell me what to expect about procedure if the police are involved down there."

"Geez, Paul, Marine Patrol doesn't have too much involvement with interstate. Running drugs or guns gets the FBI involved, and when the Feds and Maine CID came in on my investigation last year, Maine Marine Patrol took a backseat. We rarely get involved with homicides, and, as you know, that's what the drowning case turned into."

Paul nodded, his face showing his disappointment. "Yeah, I remember that all too well."

Remi stood silent for a minute. "But maybe I could call in a favor," he said. "There's a good man who worked with me on the investigation before it went wild. He's Bureau of Criminal Investigation here, and he may have some information about the bureau in Florida. I'll check with him when we get back to

68

Ocean Park."

Remi stood and clasped Paul's shoulder. "Later, Paul, okay?"

"Leaving so soon?" Jacques asked.

"Yes, sir. I've got to try and move Clare along." Remi's mouth twitched in a crooked smile aimed at Paul. "Clare's cooking supper tonight at my place." Remi reached out to shake Jacques's hand. "It's good to see you again, Professor. Take care."

They sat in silence on the porch as light faded from the sky. Jacques sipped his scotch, waiting for Margaret's call to dinner, and Paul stared at the ebbing tide, his thoughts shifting with the rhythm of the waves. Finally, Paul broke the silence. "I meant to tell you about Rafferty's call before Remi and Clare came, and I'm sorry I broke it to you the way I did, Pa."

"No need to apologize. That you are able to take the trip is the important issue. I know you have a lot to think about, but the doctor's decision you used as an excuse could be a more realistic solution than you imagine. You should have a medical opinion, Paul."

"I don't think so. The stalling wasn't about my leg. My leg only hurts when I overdo, and I'm learning how to pace myself. I worried a little about it at first, but I don't actually have a doctor appointment until the beginning of June. I stalled to give me time to convince myself that I could go down there and . . . and be productive."

Jacques raised an eyebrow but said nothing.

Paul cast a sideways glance, his thoughts in overdrive. *His eyes seem full of suspicion.* "I checked out the provenance on the painting this afternoon. That's the art history of the painting, Pa, in case you're wondering. I should have done that more thoroughly when it first came into the gallery, but I was green in a director's job." *I can't tell him about Suzanne.*

Paul paused and looked out to sea. "I think I'll know if the painting that turned up in Sarasota is the real thing, but identifying it worries me. I haven't had enough experience."

"Your discernment is not what concerns me, son. I worry that you're putting yourself in harm's way down there. When they stole the painting, you were the one shot at, so if you show up again and—"

Margaret's voice calling through the screen door cut Jacques's words short. "You-hoo, out there. Dinner is ready."

Jacques rose with a weary sigh. "We'll talk more later, Paul. It's best not to keep Margaret waiting. She's sure to have taken time to fix this meal according to Hoyle, if you get my meaning."

Paul shot Margaret a sly smile. "The fish was very tasty, Auntie Mame. Did Clare give you some tips before she left?"

Margaret was scrubbing pans while Paul sat at the kitchen table. She turned to him with an indignant look, pointing a soapy finger in his direction. "You've got it wrong way 'round. I'm the one who taught Clare how to cook."

"Just teasing, Auntie Mame." Paul tapped his finger on the information sheets that Clare brought. "I thought maybe she had some words of wisdom about a new diet for Pa."

"*Oui,* she did talk about meals and menus using the nutrition guide, but our discussion was mostly about me, eh—trying to make her understand why I had my hair colored and cut."

"And?"

Margaret grinned impishly. "I told her: when you sweep the stairs, you start at the top."

Paul laughed, giving Margaret a thumbs-up. "Way to go. But, then, how did you really explain it?"

Margaret rinsed and turned the last pan bottom-side-up on a tea towel spread on the counter. She wiped her hands on her apron and sat at the table beside Paul. "I told Clare maybe I'm just tired of people thinking I'm old-fashioned."

"Well, I don't think you're old-fashioned."

"What about your papa? He has a beautiful young wife—"

"And she can't hold a candle to you, *Tante*. Besides, Pa wouldn't have asked you here if you weren't very special to him." Paul studied his folded hands on the tabletop. "And to me."

He turned his face up to hers and cleared his throat. "That leads to something I have to talk about, *Tante*. I told Pa that I've made my decision to go to Florida, and now he's worried about me being in danger down there. He doesn't think I should go."

Paul's hands were clasped tightly on the table, and Margaret put her hand over his and kept it there.

"When I told you about Suzanne and the painting, I didn't tell you everything. I didn't talk about my suspicions." He hesitated, a muscle in his jaw twitching. "I have reason to think my friend Suzanne may have been involved in the theft, and I have to find her to know the truth."

"Does your papa know about these suspicions?"

"No, *Tante*. You are the only person who knows Suzanne exists. Not my sister, not Pa. No one else knows about her, and I want to keep it that way."

"*Mon Dieu!* Not tell your family?"

"Not now, no. Pa is stressed out as it is, and there's no need to involve anyone else in my personal life."

Margaret narrowed her eyes. "But you are involving me. There must be more about this woman than you've told me. Maybe she was *votre amoureuse,* your sweetheart, eh?"

Paul closed his eyes, pinching his lips closed.

"She left you . . . you were robbed, so maybe you blame her, eh, and you seek revenge?"

"No, *Tante*. It's not like that."

"When you seek revenge, you dig two graves. One for yourself, Jacques Paul."

"It's complicated. Suzanne may be involved." Paul removed his hands from the table and ran his fingers through his hair. "I want the painting back, but I'm certainly *not* after revenge."

Margaret cocked her head, keeping her eyes locked on his. "Then what are you after?"

Paul could feel his heart beating as seconds passed while he weighed her question. "I have feelings for Suzanne, but I can't let them get in the way. I have to know the truth about the painting."

"And you think I can help you find the truth?"

"Yes," he said, making no effort to avoid her gaze. "I do."

Margaret sighed. "I think I know what you are asking, *mon chéri,* but there is something you are not telling me." She pointed to her heart. "I feel it here."

Paul nodded and drew a deep breath. "Suzanne's father was an art dealer. Not an honest one. He was arrested and imprisoned earlier this year for selling forged copies of masterworks. Very valuable paintings." Paul's lips drew a thin line. "And Monet's *Red Boats* could be one of them. No one can know about this, yet, *Tante,* understand?"

"*Mère de Dieu,*" she whispered.

"If you could just see the painting, or Suzanne . . . maybe . . ."

Margaret was shaking her head. "Impossible, Jacques Paul. You will be in Florida, and I am here with your papa."

CHAPTER ELEVEN

Paul stood in front of his closet staring at a linen sport coat that he thought might work with summer slacks he hadn't worn in a year. He threw up his hands in a futile gesture that immediately reminded him of *Tante*. She had an expressive way of using her hands, a mannerism that was familiar and dear to him. Words popped into his mind, words his mother said long ago. "The French talk with their hands, but you and I will use our hands to create."

Paul stared at his outstretched fingers. "A hell of a mess is what these hands created."

He dragged a suitcase out of the closet and opened it near his dresser. Paul pulled drawers out one at a time, staring at the contents, trying to remember what clothes would do for Florida. *I have no problem packing shorts and jeans and T-shirts for warm weather down there, but that would not be what a respectable gallery director would wear.* Suddenly he remembered something. Back at the closet he pushed the slacks and jackets to one side and reached way in the back to a hanger still enclosed in a plastic cleaner's bag. Three silk shirts, classy yet casual. "Perfect," he said to himself, hanging them next to his linen sport coat.

Jacques drove carefully out of the medical building parking lot, brooding over what the vascular surgeon had said. Man of few words, he thought; these young professionals haven't been given much in the way of diplomacy or counseling skills.

He drove straight to Madelaine's condo, his mind waffling between the surgeon's words and Paul's decision.

A clay pot brimming with spring flowers beside the Donovans' door produced a smile on his face. It was not easy to keep the smile when Maddy opened the door. She looked so much like her mother that sadness overwhelmed him whenever he gazed into those green eyes. He closed his eyes to give her a hug.

"Papa! What a nice surprise. I was fixing a cup of tea. Will you have some with me?"

"Yes, that might settle my nerves a bit. I thought you'd be home from Saint David's by now. Is Patrick home yet?"

"No, he rarely leaves the shop before four-thirty, and I usually use this after-school time to work on lesson plans for tomorrow." Maddy steered him toward the kitchen. "That can wait, Papa. Tell me, what has you so frazzled? Was it the consultation with the surgeon?"

Jacques sat at the kitchen table while Maddy poured his tea. "Yes, that's part of it."

"What did he recommend?"

"Well, he was a very direct person. He said the surgery was needed, and I should let him know when I'm ready. It was almost like a recorded message you get on the phone, very impersonal."

"Paul told me about Doc Halliday's option for you, the meds he ordered and your diet. Did you tell the surgeon about that?"

"He knew that from my records. Doc Halliday faxed everything to him. His opinion was distressing to me for more reasons than one, Madelaine. It complicates the whole situation with your brother. Has Paul told you about Florida?"

"He told me about the call from Sean Rafferty."

Jacques sighed. "I think Paul is going to accept Rafferty's offer and fly down there. I know it's a tough predicament he's facing, but I don't think he's thinking about the danger he could be in."

"Paul is a survivor, Papa. He came out of that job in New York City and didn't give up. He found success at Cornerstone Gallery, and I think he'll be up for whatever happens in Florida."

"I hope you're right, my dear." Jacques toyed with his teacup, then turned his face up to Maddy's. "Would you come to dinner tomorrow night, Madelaine? The weekend is only two days away, and maybe talking about the trip would be a good thing. I know it's Paul's decision, but a little family input might be just what's needed."

Maddy smiled. "I understand your need to be protective, Papa, and, yes, we'll gladly come to dinner, but I doubt Paul's plans will be altered by anything Patrick or I will say." She raised her eyebrows and placed her hand on his arm. "On the other hand, when Paul hears what the surgeon had to say to you today, that might change things."

"That's exactly what makes this a thorny dilemma. I don't think Paul should go, but I won't have him change his plans because of me."

Margaret paced the porch from one end to the other. Sunrise lit the sky with amber light, tipping the waves pink and gold, but she barely took notice of the dawn. The ocean was an anathema that she tolerated only as it related to the people in this house. She never got over her anger with the sea for claiming her husband's life.

Outside the house, she pulled the hood of her jacket up over her head. She didn't like the morning damp, but she hoped the sea breeze would clear the foggy notions from her mind. Maybe she would hear a whisper on the wind of things to come. She often sensed things that were about to happen. Sometimes she tried to banish the thoughts that came to mind, but this time she really wanted to be listening.

Margaret paused by the screen door, eyes looking north toward Biddeford Pool village. *That's the shore path Grandmére took bringing Madelaine back to this century, back to Francois's Fancy. Grandmére gave Madelaine signs to find Fiona. A vision might allow me to recognize what is most important now.*

She closed her eyes, hoping for a sign. Seconds ticked by until she opened her eyes to the sky. The rising sun shone on the hilts of two crossed swords piercing the clouds. Paul and Jacques. She blinked, and the swords were gone.

Music somewhere in the house suddenly jarred her thoughts. She opened the door, looking left and right as she followed the sound down the hall to the kitchen. Musical ringing came from the cell phone she had left on the kitchen table. *No one knows I have this but Paul—Can't be.* She picked up the little phone, opened it, and the musical tone stopped.

"*Tante?* I thought you'd be up or I wouldn't be calling this early. I'm on my way to work."

"How did you know to call me on this phone, Clare Margaret? I don't even know the number yet myself!"

"Paul told me about it yesterday. Not to worry, Mom. I called to give you a heads-up. Remi and I are coming out to the Pool after work today. We have something special to tell you about, and Remi wants you to tell Paul that he found some information for him. Gotta run now. See you later, okay?"

"*Oui,* but how do I turn this thing off?" Margaret could hear Clare laughing, and that only added to her frustration.

"Just press 'end' and close it up, *Tante.*"

Margaret clicked it shut and put the cell phone back on the table, none too gently. "Jacques Paul has explaining to do," she said, shaking her finger at the phone. Her annoyance tempered as she stared at the kitchen clock. *Something special to tell me about. Good news, j'espére.*

All was quiet in the house. Breakfast passed without incident. Paul went through the how-tos with the cell phone for Margaret, did some sketching out on the porch, then retreated to the study with his laptop right after lunch. Jacques left to spend most of the day at the university, foregoing lunch at home.

Margaret busied herself planning and preparing for dinner. The dining table was set for five. Roast chicken with stuffing and two vegetables should do it. Jacques shouldn't eat the stuffing, but Patrick and Paul surely would. Peach crisp for dessert because the young people really liked that, and Jacques would agree that he didn't want them to suffer his restrictions.

She was peeling peaches when the back door opened. Clare and Remi strolled in carrying a picnic basket between them.

"What's this?" Margaret said. "It's not warm enough in May for picnics."

"Hi, *Tante*," Clare said. "No picnic, just some nibbles I made last night and . . . ta-da ta-da!" She paused as Remi pulled a bottle of champagne out of the basket. "Bubbly for a little celebration!"

Margaret's jaw dropped open. "A celebration?"

"You tell her, Remi," Clare said as she placed a bowl of cheese twists on the table.

Remi broke a wide smile. "We've set a wedding date, *Tante*, and we want you to be the first to know," he said.

Margaret dropped the peach and paring knife. She paused no longer than a second before standing on her tiptoes to kiss Remi's cheek. Then she grabbed Clare and held her close. "*Mére de Dieu, ma chérie.* I've been waiting forever for this."

Tears came to Clare's eyes and she laughed through her tears. "Me too, Mom."

"I thought I heard some commotion out here. What's going on?" Paul quipped as he entered the kitchen.

Remi and Clare spoke as one. "We've set a wedding date."

"Good God Almighty! That calls for a celebration."

"That's what we're about to do," Remi said, as he peeled the foil from the champagne bottle. "Celebrate!"

Tante grabbed a clean tea towel from the counter and handed it to Remi. "When the cork pops, just in case. Okay?" She hurried to the pantry and came back with four wine glasses.

Clare's tears were nonstop. She wiped them away with her fingers. "These are happy tears, Paul," she said as her arm went around Margaret's shoulder. "What would we do without my *tante*, huh?"

When the cork pulled out with a pop, Paul clapped Remi's shoulder. "Hey, Sarge. Gotta have a toast for champagne. Actually, I know one that's a combination of two favorite toasts I've heard. May I propose one?"

Remi nodded as he poured. "Please do."

Paul raised his glass and cleared his throat. "To two special people. There are good ships and there are wood ships, the ships that sail the sea, but the best ships are friendships and may they always be. I wish you warm words on a cold evening, a full moon on a dark night, and the road downhill all the way to your door."

"I liked that, Jacques Paul," Margaret said, "but I would add, 'And God's blessing for many children' to your toast. I will be so happy to be a *grandmére* someday!"

Clare was quick to respond. With a sparkle in her eye, she mimicked Margaret's French accent. "Well, I do have some of your *grandmère*'s genes, eh, *Tante?* You were eighth child with seven brothers, *mais oui?*"

Margaret's *"oui"* was lost in Remi's resounding "Whoa!"

In the laughter that followed, a car was heard rolling into the driveway. "Pa is missing all this. That must be him," Paul said.

"He said he'd be back by four, and it's almost that. I'll get a glass for him," *Tante* said.

Remi pulled a paper from his pocket. "Better give you this before I forget, Paul. It's the info you'll need about the Sarasota Bureau of Investigation. Names and phone numbers for connections down there came from my friend. He's listed at the top, in case you need to check with him about anything."

"When will you be leaving, Paul?" Clare asked.

"In one more day. I fly out Saturday morning, God willing," he said.

Paper in one hand, Paul shook it at Remi. "Geez, Sarge, I'm real thankful for this, and doubly glad you two finally decided to tie the knot." Paul tipped his glass and tossed back the champagne in one swallow.

Chapter Twelve

Jacques stood in the kitchen doorway, a puzzled look on his face. "Looks like a party in my house. Did I miss someone's birthday?"

Clare greeted him with a hug. "It is a very impromptu party, Papa Jacques, meant to be a surprise for *Tante,* but it wouldn't be a celebration without you. We were hoping you'd get home." Remi poured a glass of champagne for Jacques.

Jacques looked from one to the other of the smiling faces. "Is this an occasion I've forgotten about, Margaret?"

"Non, mon ami." Tante said smiling and pointing a finger at Clare. "It's for Clare and Remi to say."

Clare's face shone with a brilliant smile. She moved into the circle of Remi's arm and he nodded, holding her close. "We came to announce our wedding date! It will be June fourteenth."

"Mère de Dieu!" Tante said. "That's only weeks away. How can we plan?"

"It's all decided, Mom. We want a small wedding at Saint Mary's out here. Just family and a few close friends, then a reception, probably at King's Castle Inn." She looked up into Remi's eyes. "We're sure the Windspirits will approve."

Remi hugged her close, kissing the top of her head. "We decided on that date because it's a Saturday, and it's my birthday. Never mind that Clare says we're on opposite poles of the zodiac. We have a lot of good stuff going between us."

"Man! You'll have a whopper of an anniversary when it comes

around. A wedding and a birthday—double *entendre!* That calls for a special toast, wouldn't you say, Pa?" Paul asked.

"Of course. Let me sit for a minute and catch my breath. This is such a wonderful surprise."

Margaret sat beside him, fanning herself with a napkin. "*Eh, bien.* Take your time, Jacques. Sit everyone," she said, her flattened, outstretched hands pressing up and down in the air over the table. "All this excitement has my heart going bumpity-bump. Too much surprise in one day!" *Tante* raised an eyebrow and shot a warning look to Paul, but he remained quiet and didn't rise to her bait.

Jacques cupped his glass in hand, staring at the pale golden liquid. "I had to gather my thoughts for a minute, but I'm ready, now." More seconds passed as he looked at Margaret, then back at Clare and Remi. Jacques raised his glass. "They say that when children find true love, parents find true joy. I hope that is true for you, Margaret, and for the Windspirits. Remi and Clare, my greatest wish for you is that through the years your love for each other will deepen and grow, and that years from now you will look back on your wedding day as the day you loved each other the least."

Silence filled the room and once more Clare brushed tears from her eyes. "Thank you, Papa Jacques," she said. "That was beautiful."

Jacques rose. "I really must go upstairs and rest before dinner. It was a long day finishing end-of-semester duties. You will all be relieved to know, as I was, that suspicious allegations and inquiries have been dropped in the investigation of my student's death. It was revealed that he had a rare bone disease and was overmedicating himself with pain prescriptions. On a happier note, Madelaine and Patrick are coming tonight, and of course you two are more than welcome to stay for dinner." Jacques clasped Clare and Remi's hands in each of his across the table before he turned to leave the room. "Your announcement has brightened my day."

Clare and Remi did not stay for dinner. Paul was convinced they fled the barrage of questions that *Tante* began to fling because they hadn't yet considered all the wedding details she brought up. Sweet Jesus! What would he do in their shoes? Probably the same thing.

Big weddings were too dammed costly. Odds were, if it was him, he might even elope—with the right woman. The right woman. He came close to telling everyone at the dinner table about Suzanne. Maddy's questions about what happened in the days before the break-in were hard to slough off. *Tante*'s piercing glances were not easily ignored either, and that was reason enough for him to keep mum. There would be no disclosures about Suzanne Petrone. Not yet.

Jacques repeated his concerns about criminals, a gun hired to do away with a witness suddenly showing up in Florida. "You can't be cavalier about that," he'd warned.

Huh-uh. Cavalier he was not. Scared was more like it. The question beating in his mind: how much to tell Rafferty's private eye about Suzanne. He would definitely need an investigator to find her. No two ways about it. Hell, the cops probably already had the book on her connection to Anthony Petronelli.

Would Suzanne have taken the Monet from her father's forgery collection—instead of from the largesse of a French dealer who bargained for more than her trust? That was the bigger question, but it was a problem for another day.

"Clare will be a married woman. *Aye yi yi.*" Head in her hands, Margaret slumped at the table and spoke the words aloud to the empty kitchen, her mind a muddle of thoughts. "What to do? *Laisse allez!* 'Let go, let go,' my Jean would say, whenever

Clare wanted her independence. *Oui,* I did that and Clare never let me down. But, now, there is so little time!" Margaret waggled her head, worry played across her face.

What a muddle life is, she thought. *But first things first.* She picked up the wooden spoon from the array of whisks and spoons she had spread on the table, and tapped lightly on the oak tabletop. Tap, tap. *First, I have to take good care of Jacques until Kathleen returns.* Trés bien, *I can cook for him and ease his worries. Didn't I help* granmére *cook for my seven brothers and my papa?*

I used to grumble and was resentful I had no mother or sisters to help with all the chores, but Papa would say, "If you harbor bitterness, happiness will dock elsewhere." I learned to be grateful for my hands to serve and, best of all, thankful that I learned to cook like my granmére. *She was* cusinier magnifique.

Margaret waggled her head with the tap, tap of the spoon. *Next, Jacques Paul needs help, but time is not on my side, nor his.* Mon Dieu, *his troubles, like the sea, are bounded, and I worry he won't make it through alone.* She tossed the spoon into a bowl and began to assemble the rest of the ingredients for maple sugar cakes to pack for Paul's plane trip. He said they get nothing but peanuts on the plane.

Late night, Friday, May 9

A sickle moon was climbing the sky, shedding weak light to his bedroom. Fitful sleep came slowly. Ghostly figures haunted Paul's dream. Papa was at the helm, his mother, Julie, close beside him at the stern rail. They were riding giant waves in a phantom sailing ship, her sword-like bowsprit, the full-breasted figurehead of Suzanne, black hair streaming to the forecastle. The bowsprit would disappear in waves that broke over the bow, then reappear, Suzanne's presence very real in the darkness that overwhelmed him.

Paul awoke slowly, shapes clarifying in the light of a pale dawn. He turned off the alarm. *Sweet Jesus, what a nightmare, and only two hours before departure.* He tested his bad leg, walking barefoot without a cane to the bathroom, his mind and stomach churning. *I've no doubt* Tante *will be ready with coffee, but more than that I can't handle this morning.*

His bag was all packed and ready at the kitchen door, with hopes that his father wouldn't hear Clare drive up. The scheme was for naught. Jacques was sitting in the kitchen in his robe and slippers talking with Margaret when Paul came downstairs. Margaret poured a cup of coffee. "I was just about to call up to you, *chérie*. What would you like to eat?"

"I'm fine with just coffee, *Tante*. Clare should be along any minute. She promised to get me to the jetport by seven."

"No breakfast? Not a good start, Jacques Paul," Margaret said, shaking her head at him.

"I'll have time to kill before departure and I may get a bite there, if I'm hungry." Paul looked at his father's solemn face. "I didn't expect you to be up, Pa. I thought we said our good-byes."

"We did, but I didn't say all that I wanted to say last night." His eyes clouded with weariness as he drained his cup. "Last night I was hoping against odds for a change of mind. In the clear light of dawn I knew that was wishful thinking. I'm still against your going, but I wanted you to know my feelings." Jacques tried to smile. "You know that old adage, 'caution is the better part of valor'? I'm hoping that you will be cautious, son. Do not hesitate to call here for any reason."

Jacques stood and grasped Paul's shoulders. "Remember that I will be praying that God strengthens you when you need to be strong. I love you, son." This was something Jacques rarely said. His words were raspy as he whispered a blessing, *"Dieu Bénisent."* He nodded at Margaret and abruptly left the kitchen.

Margaret put her hands on her hips, opened her mouth to speak and closed it quickly when the door opened and Clare bustled in. "Mornin', Mom. Sunrise today promises a good day for a flight. No pink sky in the mornin'. All set, Cap?"

Margaret looked from one to the other. "Leaving already? I thought your flight was at eight-ten," Margaret said.

"It is, but I have to check in at least forty-five minutes ahead, and Clare has to get back to town for first shift." He gulped his coffee and leaned to kiss Margaret's cheek. "Don't hesitate to use that cell phone like I told you." He looked Margaret straight in the eye. "I expect direct communication from my lady. Will you promise me that?"

"Oui, I promise, *cheri,"* Margaret said, flustered by everything happening so fast. She removed a plastic sandwich bag from a bread box on the counter. "I almost forgot. Sugar cakes for the trip, eh. Put them in your pocket, Jacques Paul."

CHAPTER THIRTEEN

Clare's sunrise prediction didn't hold true. One hour into the flight they hit a storm, delaying US Airways' arrival in Charlotte. It was a tight connection, but Paul tipped a porter to put him in an electric car with two handicapped passengers. They zipped from one gate to the other and boarded on time. The second half of the trip was smooth. The pilot made up time, arriving at Tampa International at one o'clock.

It was easy to spot the man sent to the airport to meet Paul. Mr. Rafferty had told him to expect a man in his thirties, medium height, rail thin, with close-cropped rust-colored hair and matching mustache. The clincher would be a vivid green feather stuck in his straw hat. *It has to be him.* Paul struggled not to smirk as he eyed the hat.

The man cocked one rusty eyebrow when Paul stuck out his hand. "JP?"

"That's right," Paul said, trying to gaze straight at the man's blue eyes instead of the ridiculous feather in his hat. It was hard to keep from smiling, despite the serious look on the other's face.

"Name's Daniel. If you've no other luggage to get, then follow me. We'll be takin' the elevator to the parking garage."

"This bag is it," Paul said, pulling it along on wheels. *Clipped and kind of formal, trace of an accent—not even sure this is my man.*

Daniel didn't speak again until they were inside a late-model silver BMW. "Nice wheels," Paul said. "Yours?"

"No," Daniel said in a distinct Scottish burr that made the word *no* sound like *new*. "And the feather wasn't my idea." He tossed the feather into the glove compartment and adjusted his hat. "I was told to use Mr. Rafferty's vehicle to pick you up. He keeps it at Winter House year-round, along with a housekeeper and anything else a body'd be needin' when they stay at the Key."

"The Key? What key? I thought we were going to Sarasota."

"We will be." Daniel gave Paul a sideways glance. "Tomorrow. We're just passing through the southern end of Sarasota this trip. Winter House is on Casey Key."

Winter House . . . not a very imaginative name, and this guy doesn't fit my picture of a PI. Paul stifled a yawn.

"You weary, JP?"

Paul did a mental eye roll. "Mr. Rafferty used my initials for an easy ID for you, but I prefer Paul, and, yes, I'm tired. Been up since dawn."

"Might as well snooze, then, Paul. I'll nudge you when we get to the exit for Sarasota."

Paul didn't get nudged until they were south of Sarasota. "Heads up, man. Getting close. We're waiting on a swing bridge to get to the island—this bridge is interesting to watch, dates back to the nineteen-twenties. They say it's one of only two left in the state."

Paul watched as a man came out of a little gatehouse and stood on the bridge as it swung to the right like a slow carnival ride. A green sign—"Blackburn Point"—came into view attached to the north side of the bridge. From where their car idled, the tip of a fishing boat was visible passing through the channel. The bridge swung back, the man got off, and they were on their way.

"I've seen drawbridges, but never one of those."

Daniel merely nodded and pointed to a sign as he made a left turn at a dead end, Casey Key Road.

"This is it?" Paul asked.

"The Key is a barrier island eight miles long, and Winter House is less than halfway down this road."

Palm trees and lush tropical growth shaded a narrow, winding road. Paul had glimpses of private enclaves on either side, some half hidden behind wrought-iron gates, glimpses of imposing entrances behind flowering bushes and vines. Several were towering Mediterranean-style palaces built on pilings and walled in. Paul's head swiveled from bayside docks on the bay left, to sandy beaches and blue Gulf waters on the right. "This looks like a secluded paradise for the rich and famous," he said.

"Not far from right, aye. It's strictly residential till you get to the southern end. Some residents keep their own private jets nearby, but not Mr. Rafferty. He may be rich as Croesus, but he doesn't flaunt it. The missus likes the location for its privacy and proximity to the arts and culture in Sarasota, himself for the tennis club at the next key up. That would be Siesta Key."

Daniel turned into a sand-and-shell driveway banked with bougainvillea on the Gulf side of the road. Paul's eye caught a small bronze plaque—"Seaview"—that sat atop a carved dolphin on a cedar post. "I thought you called this place Winter House." They waited while the garage door opened.

"Aye, I did. That's what Mr. Rafferty chooses to call it. He never bothered to change the sign left here by former owners. Folks on this road still think of this place as Seaview, and himself likes it that way. He bought the place and did a major renovation three years ago so the missus could enjoy a warm climate for the winter months, and he could play tennis year-round."

By this time Daniel had pulled into a garage and parked next to a compact dark blue Ford. He hefted Paul's bag from the trunk and trekked with it to the front of a small elevator.

Paul's steps slowed. Although a fan whirred overhead, he was suddenly aware of the change in climate. Everything so far had been air-conditioned. He took off his sport coat, folded it over his arm and entered the elevator with Daniel, more than amazed by everything he'd seen.

"Winter House is mostly for family use, but occasionally Mr. Rafferty sends a guest down." Daniel quirked one red eyebrow at Paul as the elevator door opened. "But you, JP, don't quite fit either category, eh?"

Paul didn't know how to react to that question, but it didn't matter, because Daniel didn't wait for an answer. He exited the elevator and put Paul's bag down next to a breakfast bar counter that circled the kitchen where he stood.

Paul paused beside him. The sight before him was a breath-taking panorama. Opposite the ultramodern open kitchen stretched a spacious living room. Glass doors at the far end were open to a terrace and pool, and beyond the terrace, steps led down to a sandy beach edging the endless blue water of the Gulf of Mexico.

A woman sitting at the far end of the kitchen counter slipped off a bar stool and came toward them. "Well now, Daniel," she said, "you didn't give me a heads-up like you were supposed ta. And why not?" she asked in a lilting Irish brogue.

Daniel broke into a smile, the first Paul had seen. "Never mind, Molly. We're here, aye? My passenger slept while we traveled, and I didn't choose to wake him. This is JP, er . . . Paul Fontaine. Meet Molly O'Brien, Mr. Rafferty's housekeeper."

"Pleased to meet you, sir," she said. A warm smile dimpled her cheeks and lit her bright brown eyes, reminding him instantly of *Tante* Margaret.

"My pleasure," Paul said, smiling back.

"Are you hungry or thirsty, Mr. Fontaine?"

"Please, call me Paul." He looked around, noting arched

hallways to the left and right of the wide living room. Fans whirred overhead. "I'd like to shed this coat and use the bathroom. Can you tell me where to do that?"

"Sure, and I have a room all ready for you. Come along, this way." Molly pursed her lips, giving Daniel a sideways look that seemed to speak annoyance. She moved to the hall on the left side of the living room. "I've put you in the front, so you have a grand view. My quarters are just here behind you." She pointed to a door opposite the one she paused by. "Take your ease, dearie. I'll be in the kitchen till dinner time, and if you're missing anything you need, just give a call."

Molly opened the door and stepped aside as Paul entered. He heard it snick shut behind him. Glass doors at the far end of the bedroom opened to the terrace that stretched across the front of the house. A sitting area, a private bath, and a queen-sized bed. *Damn, if this isn't a suite, not just a room!*

Paul opened a closet to hang his coat and found hats on a shelf, panamas, peaked tennis caps and floppy beach hats. He opened his bag, pulled out his toiletry kit and a clean polo shirt and stashed his suitcase on a low rack next to flip-flops and beach sandals. *Daniel pegged it right. Everything a body needs.* Same thing in the bathroom: soaps, shampoo, lotions and thick towels were stacked on recessed marble shelves beside the shower.

He was stepping out of the bathroom when his cell phone rang. He'd called Jacques just as the plane landed in Tampa, so it couldn't be him. "Hello."

"Sean Rafferty here. Daniel tells me you arrived on time, JP, and Molly has you settled in. I trust everything is satisfactory at Winter House?"

"More than satisfactory, sir. I never expected—"

"Make yourself comfortable and count on Molly to pamper you. She loves to do just that. Meantime, I suggest you follow

Daniel's lead. Trust him explicitly. You'll find he's good at what he does. He will keep me informed, but you can also ask Molly to reach me in case of an emergency. We have an additional line here, just for Winter House. Good luck, JP."

Paul heard the click before he could say his thanks or ask a question. He pocketed his phone and walked out onto the terrace. A small grove of palm trees and a tall, thick hedge of yellow, flowering bushes shielded the terrace from the next property. Sea oats waved in the breeze at the edge of the sand, and pelicans flew east overhead toward the bay. Paul looked up to follow their flight and noticed the cedar-shake roof. *Probably the single architectural token of Rafferty's New England roots.* It didn't look as out of place as Paul felt in Sean Rafferty's tropical paradise.

He walked past lounges and umbrella tables surrounding the pool and spa before entering the living room. Three contemporary paintings effectively grouped on the nearest wall caught his eye. Sand dunes and aquamarine water, a sailboat race, and a spectacular Gulf sunset, each painting signed and dated "R. Brant 06".

"Those are Mrs. R's selections," Molly said, gesturing with a chopping knife from the kitchen island. "The missus bought them from a local artist who has a studio at the south end of the Key. She likes his work."

"I'd say Mrs. Rafferty made excellent choices. I like his style. It's a man, you say?"

" 'Tis a man, yes, but I'd venture to say you'll be seein' lots more famous paintings than those, tomorrow. Leastwise, that's what Daniel's got planned, the good Lord willing."

Paul ambled into the kitchen and sat on one of the bar stools facing Molly. "Is he here somewhere? I haven't had a chance to talk with Daniel about any plans."

"No, dearie. He'll be back shortly, though. He's a quiet one,

Daniel is. Very smart, and he knows the area very well, be sure of that. He'll take you where ya need to go." She paused to place chopped vegetables into a large salad bowl. "Now, can I fix you a cocktail or a cold drink, Paul? I have some nibbles I'll bring out to the terrace, if you like."

"A cold beer will be fine, if you have one." Thinking she seemed determined to wait on him, Paul accepted the beer from her hand, thanked her and took himself out to one of the umbrella tables. He had barely tipped the bottle before Molly brought a tray of peeled shrimp, crackers and cheese.

"You'll be getting a double taste of the sea today. Dinner's at six, and we're havin' grouper tonight. I hope it's to yer liking"— she beamed an infectious smile at him—"I just couldn't resist letting you try our shrimp. These are fresh from the gulf, they are."

Paul dipped a shrimp into sauce, nodding his head as he chewed. "Delicious. We don't get shrimp like this in Maine, but we do have fresh lobster. Ever been to Maine, Molly?"

"No, but I've heard about it from the missus. I came to Florida from Boston four years ago, same as Daniel. Would you believe we was born in the same county in Ireland?"

"I guessed Ireland from your accent, Molly, but Daniel doesn't sound quite like you. You have a soft lilt to your voice."

"Daniel lived in Scotland with his mum until he came to the States; spent his teen years in Boston, though. His mum is Mr. Rafferty's sister."

Paul leaned back in a lounge chair, folded his hands behind his head, and stared out to sea. His mind held so many questions. Molly filled in some of the blanks, but there were so many unanswered ones that he didn't know where to begin. Should he start with the contacts Remi gave him, or should he follow Daniel's lead as Rafferty advised?

Daniel came back in time for dinner, but there was little chance for answers. Molly tended to dominate the conversation as they sat together at the long table.

"Oh, yes. I'm to eat with you as though this was my residence." Molly laughed heartily at her own words. " 'Course I do live here, so 'tis my residence while I'm workin' for Mr. R, wouldn't you say?"

Daniel looked at Paul from under heavy red eyebrows. "We're all working for *Mr. R.* Isn't that so, Paul?"

That was a quirky way to put it. "In a sense, you're right. Sean Rafferty does own Cornerstone Gallery."

Paul complimented Molly on a fine meal, but she shooed him out to the terrace. "Daniel helps me in the kitchen after dinner, so put your leg up and rest it, dearie, or you'll not be keeping up with Daniel tomorrow."

Another *Tante* was all Paul could think of. Another take-charge person. No wonder Rafferty kept her here full-time. Molly excused herself and headed for her room soon after the kitchen work was done, and Daniel joined Paul on the terrace.

"Molly tells me you came here when Mr. Rafferty opened the house in two thousand four."

"Aye, we came to help the family settle in."

"You're not year-round in Florida, though, are you?"

"No, just Molly is. Generally, I'm here only on assignment, or during the season when *himself* needs some special services. I stayed longer than usual in oh-four because of the robbery."

"A robbery here? What was stolen?"

"Some paintings brought from Boston and a few pieces of jewelry. Pretty selective and professional thieves, they were. No prints left. The bastards were slick and slippery as eels."

"Did the police find them?"

"Not until they tried to fence the paintings up in Georgia two months later. That's how I learned the ropes down here. I'd just started working as a PI before we left Boston, and this case kind of fell into my lap from the boss. The local police reached a dead end in February, and I got lucky."

"Are you saying *you* ended up finding the stolen goods?"

"Not quite. A tip came from an artist that the paintings showed up for barter on the black market. As you may know, Paul, some artists are on the shaky end of deals. There's dishonesty in every profession."

"I don't doubt that." *Is this leading to Suzanne?*

"Interstate trafficking across state lines brought the Feds in. Rubbing shoulders with the agents in the district office taught me a lot, but it was a local artist who got that tip. He had a gallery in Sarasota. Turned out to be a lucky lead."

Rafferty said follow his lead. . . . "You said *had* a gallery in Sarasota. You mean the artist is no longer there?"

"That's right. At least not physically. He still sends his work to a co-op gallery in Sarasota, but he opened his own place right here on the Key in oh-five."

Paul's head swiveled to the paintings on the living-room wall. He pointed at the grouping. "Molly says those paintings are by a local artist that Mrs. Rafferty likes. Would that be—"

"One and the same. Robert Brant. Hell of a nice guy." Daniel pointed to the sun that was dropping in a cloudless sky. "About fifteen minutes to go. Want to catch sunset from the Cove? It's a tiki bar just five minutes down to the south end, and we might even see Brant there. I'm told he's there on an occasional Friday night."

"Sounds good to me."

They drove in Daniel's Ford sports coupe. Near the beaches, the properties became more commercial. Guest houses, typical beach cottages, and in between, a few shops. One of them stood out, a vivid green-and-yellow-painted building, backlit by the fading sunlight. "That's Brant's shop. If we don't see him at the

Cove, we'll catch him at his studio another day."

Brant wasn't at the Cove. The two watched from the open tiki hut as the sun descended into the Gulf like a fiery orange ball. Surprised when Daniel ordered a single-malt scotch, Paul threw a twenty on the bar. "Make it two," he said.

Daniel nodded to the bartender as the drinks were served. "Evenin', Jake." When the bartender moved to the other end of the bar, Daniel swiveled on the bar stool to face Paul. His head was inches from Paul's face, yet he lowered his voice to a whisper. "I appreciate the offer, but you have to understand something, JP. You obviously ken Mr. Rafferty is a wealthy man, so I'm well paid for what I do, expenses included." Daniel stuffed the twenty into Paul's shirt pocket. "Most people here know I run a tab, working for Rafferty. What they don't know is he's my uncle."

Daniel was obviously waiting for a reaction, but this was not the time to reveal Molly's loose lips. Paul sipped his scotch, waiting for Daniel's next move.

CHAPTER FOURTEEN

"So you can get your bearings," Daniel said, "you need to see the whole of it first, to get the big picture." They were on Bayfront Drive in Sarasota, Daniel giving an early-morning verbal tour as they drove. He began with a description of the "cultural coast" as they headed north from Casey Key. Twenty minutes on Tamiani Trail, and Sarasota came alive before Paul's eyes, just as it was described. Concrete-and-glass buildings towered along Bayfront Drive. Sailboats moored offshore rocked in the early-morning breeze.

"Bayfront Park is just ahead. Tons of boats there and a good restaurant in the marina, but we're turning here on Main Street," Daniel said.

Paul craned his neck to look back at the busy waterfront as the car turned, but his cell-phone ring tone brought him sharply forward. He pulled the phone from his shirt pocket.

"Hallo, Jacques Paul. Am I calling too early, *cheri?*"

Paul couldn't help but smile as he glanced sideways at Daniel. "No, actually, *Tante,* early is good, except that right now I'm in a car driving through the city and the reception isn't that great."

"What? You mean I'm already messing up with this cell phone? I'm keeping my promise, but maybe I should use the house phone, eh?"

Paul smothered a laugh. "Your cell phone isn't the problem, Auntie Mame. I gave it to you so you could call me privately.

The problem is my location right now. We're in traffic, so tell me quickly, is Pa okay?"

"*Oui,* he's walking the beach this morning. I'll call back later, okay?"

"Better yet, I'll call *you* later." He clicked it shut, still smiling. "She's not really my aunt. She's an old friend staying with my father for a while. Molly reminds me a little of her, only this woman is much more than a good cook and a take-charge person."

Daniel raised his eyebrows. "What is that supposed to mean?"

"Not what you think. Margaret has second sight. She's a reluctant clairvoyant, a psychic who was raised *not* to use her powers. She's helped our family, though, in many ways. She's at our house helping while my father's wife is away, mainly because my father has a health problem and she's promised to keep me informed about him."

Daniel pulled into a parking lot behind busy Main Street. "If you're up to some walking, we're going to pass by some galleries along Palm Avenue. South Palm is historic and the stylish galleries are worth looking at. Ask away if you have any questions."

"Is one of them the gallery where the Monet was brought?"

"No. Your painting was shown to a dealer-appraiser who works for a large gallery. We may go to him later, but not today. Preliminaries first, Paul, you ken?"

Daniel's Scottish burr was beginning to grate on Paul's nerves. *Preliminaries to what?* As they meandered down to South Palm, he was impressed with the charm of the avenue and the displays in the gallery windows, but he felt like a player in a monopoly game. Make the wrong move and go directly to jail. *Maybe that's why Rafferty brought me here.*

His leg was beginning to ache, and he was relieved when they circled back to Main Street. A sidewalk café up ahead was a welcome sight. Paul mentioned coffee, and Daniel was quick to pull out a chair for him at the first awning-covered table they came to.

After they ordered, Paul gazed up the busy street. One-story shops stood next to tall, newer buildings, an eclectic mix of fine-art venues emphasizing culture with a capital C.

"The artist you told me about last night, was his gallery around here?" Paul asked.

"Actually, Brant's gallery was back on South Palm." Daniel sipped his coffee, watching Paul over the rim of his cup. "Quite near the gallery where a woman was murdered a few years back. You probably heard about that, being part of the art world, aye?"

Paul met his gaze. "I did read about that murder in the national news. Don't tell me you were involved in that case?"

The question produced a rare grin as Daniel shook his head. "It caused a great deal of panic here in the city, but, no, the murder happened in oh-four, just after Uncle moved to Casey Key. We only knew what we read in the papers." Daniel's face became serious as he paused to meet Paul's gaze. "The woman was stabbed to death as she worked in her gallery. We learned more when we met Robert Brant the following year. Rob was a person of interest in the case, bein' that the murdered gallery owner was a friend of his. Horrible crime. A butcher, the man was."

Stunned, Paul waited for the other shoe to drop. *There has to be more about Brant than he's telling.*

"All the galleries were shocked by the killing, but Brant especially was. The victim had befriended him, helped Rob get started. He was cleared, o' course, but he eventually closed up his South Palm studio and moved to the Key the following year."

Paul's mind was on overload, but he was determined to find

out where all this was leading. "This murder and mayhem story is hitting close to home, Daniel. Can we move along, now?"

"Sure." Daniel signaled the waiter. He paid the tab and pointed up Main Street. "Up there before the turn to the next avenue is the last gallery you should see before we move on. How's the leg holding up?"

"I'm sure it will get me there."

When they reached the building, Daniel paused in front of awning-covered double windows. "They say this is the oldest gallery in the city."

Beautifully arranged fine-art pieces, porcelain and raku pottery graced the window that Paul stood in front of. To his left, and centered in the next window, an easel bore a magnificent oil-on-linen portrait, a framed nude. Her pale body, the breasts high and firm, an hourglass waist and long, shapely legs were unmistakable.

Paul drew in a sharp breath. "Sweet Christ Almighty," he murmured. His eyes squinted at *R.Brant,* then widened, flashing fire at Daniel. "You knew!"

Daniel nodded. "Aye, Paul. First things first. Ye have a connection now, so next we try to find the illusive and stunning model, Miss Petrone."

Margaret stood at the south end of the porch, watching. Dusk was fast approaching, making it hard to see Jacques plodding along the shore, returning from his walk. No amount of reasoning could stop him from walking the beach twice each day. "It's my thinking and praying time," he'd said, and she couldn't argue with that.

When she saw him reach the dune path to the house, Margaret went inside to fix his scotch. Since Paul left, she'd sat with Jacques each evening before supper while he had his drink. Yesterday he'd read "The Twilight Time" to her from Robert

Browning's poetry book. *Grow old with me, the best is yet to be . . .* "It's a favorite of mine, but it's bittersweet," he'd told her, because it reminded him of Julie. No mention was made of Kathleen. Kathleen had chosen not to come home yet and that must be sad for him too.

Jacques reached the porch steps. Holding fast to the banister, he was dizzy from a sudden wave of despair—or was it his brain? He stumbled up the steps, reached for the door and darkness overcame him.

Margaret heard the thud. She found him lying across the threshold, caught between the half-open screen door. *"Bon Signeur!"* she screamed. Frightened out of her wits, she knelt beside him and put her ear to his chest. Jacques's eyes were fluttering, and he was trying to raise his head.

"I'm all right, Margaret, just a little dizzy."

"No, no, *chéri.* Lie still, Jacques. I'll get help."

He had pulled himself to a sitting position. "Just help me up, I'm not injured, Margaret. I need to get inside. Help me do that, please."

She grumbled, but did as he asked, pulled and tugged and somehow found the strength to help him stand and walk shakily into the living room.

Blustering, red-faced, she told him in no uncertain terms that she was calling Madelaine right away. He did not object.

Paul didn't want to see the rest of the city. He insisted on entering the gallery and examining the painting. Daniel went back for the car, drove to the gallery and parked outside to wait. The only new piece of information Paul found was dates. The nude of Suzanne was painted in 2007 and submitted to the gallery in March of this year.

"Where did you get your information about Suzanne?" Paul asked as they drove south out of the city.

100

"Step back a bit, Paul. You probably knew that your Monet was reported to the Stolen Art File, aye?"

"I was in the hospital when that was done, but I was made aware of it, yes."

"When the painting showed up at a dealer's in Sarasota, the dealer suspected it was a forgery. He was obligated to call the local police to investigate. The cops requested access to the Stolen Art File, and that's how the Feds got involved."

The pieces were beginning to fit. FBI must have had a file on Petronelli. The rub was that the Monet *Les bateaux rouges Argenteuil* was a suspected forgery. That was news Paul hadn't expected. Bad news, but he wasn't about to reveal anything yet. He needed that list he got from Remi before he said any more.

"You mentioned rubbing shoulders with the FBI. That's not what usually happens with private investigators from what I hear."

" 'Tisn't no." Daniel shot a sideways glance at Paul. "But then, the average PI doesn't have Sean Rafferty for an uncle." Daniel let that sit a few seconds. "Truth be known, I learned about the Petronelli connection from my friend, Rob Brant."

Brant again. Feelings welled up. *Mrs. Rafferty likes his work, Daniel calls him friend and Suzanne obviously . . .* Paul gritted his teeth and stewed in silence until he saw the sign for Casey Key.

"I'd like a one-on-one with Brant, if it can be arranged. I'd like to hear for myself what your *friend* has to say about Suzanne."

CHAPTER FIFTEEN

"So, Madelaine, did you convince your papa he should take the surgeon's advice?"

"I tried, but at least he agreed to talk again with Doctor Halliday and then Kathleen, in that order." Maddy leaned across the kitchen table, lowering her voice. "I know Papa can't hear me upstairs in his room, but these old walls"—she rolled her eyes—"you never know. I think I should wait until tomorrow to talk to Paul about this. What do you think, *Tante?*"

"I don't think your papa wants Paul to know the seriousness of this."

Maddy nodded. "Probably not. I called Clare on my way over here and asked her opinion. She says if the incidents are this frequent, it would not be wise to wait."

"Did my Clare say she was working tomorrow?"

"She didn't say, but tomorrow's Sunday and she might be off. She said something about having three days in a row next week. Patrick isn't with me tonight because he was at a meeting of the Craftsmen's Association when you called. I'm sure he would take Papa to the doctor, if he needs transportation."

"No need, *cherie.* Doctor Halliday intends to meet your papa right after his rounds at the medical center early in the morning. Doctor says he'll bring Jacques back to the Pool. I'm going in to see if Clare wants to go to church with me, eh, so I'll be driving Jacques and me to town."

★ ★ ★ ★ ★

When they arrived at the medical center, Clare wasn't there, and she didn't answer her phone at the apartment. Margaret slipped into Saint Joseph's a little late for the nine-o'clock mass. She sat in the back pew and watched everyone leave after mass, but no Clare. *I know my way to King's Castle Inn,* she thought. *Maybe Remi knows where she is.*

Margaret looked at all the cars parked up and down the road for services at the temple in Ocean Park, but a little farther on she spied what she was looking for at the rear of the inn: Remi's truck. She pulled in beside it. The closed sign didn't deter her. She walked around to the front door and rang the bell twice. Remi pulled the door curtain aside, peeked out, then opened the door.

"Mrs. Chamberlaine. What a surprise."

"Hallo, Remi. May I come in?"

Margaret's eyes looked down at his bare feet as Remi backed up to let her into the hall.

"Of course. Forgive my manners. I wasn't expecting anyone since the inn closed."

Bare-chested in a faded pair of sweats, he looked like he hadn't been awake too long, but Margaret could smell bacon cooking. "Uh-oh, I bet I'm interrupting your breakfast, eh? I'm sorry, Remi. I was looking for Clare and I thought maybe you knew . . ."

Remi rocked from one foot to the other. "Well, uh, is there something I—"

"Come on back to the kitchen," a voice called from the end of the hall, a voice definitely sounding like Clare. "Breakfast's on."

Remi looked sheepishly at Margaret, then plodded straight back, leading the way into the big kitchen at the rear of the house.

Tante could see that he was not his calm, cool self. He stopped and stood near the table, staring at Clare. She was fussing at the stove, wearing a faded oversize sweatshirt that came down to the knees of her jeans. She scooped bacon out of a pan onto paper towels. "I'm here fixing a good breakfast for Remi." She turned with a plate in her hand. "Want some eggs, *Tante?*"

Margaret was confused. "*Merci.* I've had my breakfast. I was in town looking for you to go to church with me, Clare. I tried your apartment, but you didn't answer."

Clare turned to face Margaret, a concerned look on her face. "Sorry, Mom. I thought you'd be going to church with Jacques out at the chapel. That is if he'd rallied enough to go to church. Maddy told me what happened. Is he okay?"

Margaret frowned. "I guess you couldn't know I was bringing him in to meet Doctor Halliday this morning."

"No." Clare shook her head, her eyes revealing her sadness.

"I don't know what will happen next. When I didn't find you, I went to mass, eh. I prayed for Jacques." She looked at Remi, who still stood by the table staring at Clare. "And for Remi's papa."

Clare put the plate down and moved quickly to Margaret's side. "I wish I had known," she said, putting her arm around *Tante* and pressing her cheek to Margaret's head.

Margaret pulled away. "So, now, I should be on my way. I've interrupted, and you should both sit and have your breakfast. I can find my way out."

Ignoring Clare's protest, Margaret walked quickly past Remi, out of the kitchen and out of the inn. Nagging thoughts plagued her as she drove away from Ocean Park. *Clare's car wasn't parked there.*

A bell jingled over the door of Robert Brant's studio. Daniel's rare smile greeted the man who stepped forward to shake hands.

"Daniel, my friend. Rumor has it you were leaving for Boston."

Paul was stunned by the man's physical appearance. *He looks like a damned bronze Viking.* Brant stood as tall as Paul, but muscles rippled beneath a paint-stained T-shirt when he shook Daniel's hand. His straw-colored, curly hair, streaked gold from the sun, was drawn back in a ponytail. Fine wrinkles around his eyes marked him, maybe, early forties.

"No, I'm back at Seaview for a time," Daniel said. "I've brought Paul Fontaine to meet you. He's a fellow artist, down from Portland, Maine."

Brant cast a quick look at Daniel, then back to Paul.

"Good to meet you. You must be a friend of the Raffertys?"

"Not exactly," Paul said. "I'm an employee. Interim director of Sean Rafferty's Cornerstone Gallery. At least I was until a month ago."

A look of understanding flashed across Brant's face. His lips parted with a nod of his head. "Ah. My apology. Your name didn't register at first." He raised an eyebrow at Daniel. "Do you have time for coffee?"

"I think Paul would like to talk with *you*, Rob, and I have errands to do for Molly. Say I come back in half an hour. Will that do, Paul?"

Paul nodded, glad that Daniel remembered the one-on-one he wanted with this guy. Brant hung a closed sign on the door as Daniel left. He pointed at folding screens that divided the large room they stood in. "Just behind the screens you'll find some comfortable chairs, props and things. Help yourself to coffee. I'll be right with you."

A high window threw light on the working space of the studio. Paul walked to an easel that held a work in progress, a fairly large watercolor of two children playing on a sandy beach. It evoked the memory of his mother's painting, back at Francois's

Fancy . . . he and Maddy, playing in the sand . . . years and a thousand miles ago. He studied it, comparing the style. His thoughts were jarred by Brant's voice.

"That's my sister and me when we were kids. I'm trying to finish the painting as a birthday gift for her." He removed the canvas, replacing it with one he carried. Glancing at Paul, he pointed to the easel. "This is the one we should discuss."

Surprised, Paul stared at the sketch in pastels, a profile of a woman studying a miniature painting arranged on a table. It was an unusual portrait. The woman's features, bathed in light, suggested an almost sensual joy in what she was beholding, yet the painting she studied was undefined. It was definitely Suzanne's profile.

"I sketched that from memory after I met Suzanne. She was viewing an exhibit at Ringling. I watched her from a distance and was impressed with her concentration and her visual reaction to each painting she looked at. I tried to capture that reaction in this." He paused, his hand on the portrait, fingers moving over the edges as though it held magic.

"I managed an introduction to her from the exhibiting artist." He smiled as he reminisced. "Not long after that day, we met again at a gallery on South Palm, and I invited her to come to my studio."

"And this is where the nude was painted?"

Rob Brant rubbed the back of his neck and nodded. He sat on a stool next to the easel, staring at Paul. "You always cut to the chase like that?"

The muscles in Paul's jaw twitched and his hands clenched. "It wouldn't take a genius to guess what happened between A and Z."

"Sorry to disappoint, but your guess is off the mark. It's not the way it went down. I teach a class here twice a week. Helps me stay alive. Nobody's buying art right now, but there are some pretty talented kids, future artists who are trying to get started despite the economy. I demonstrate technique with different mediums in my class for a small fee. Gives them a start and helps pay the overhead to keep me going."

Brant removed the painting from the easel, replacing it with the unfinished beach scene. He held the painting of Suzanne on his knee, tapping it with his finger. "This was my lead into what Suzanne eventually agreed to. After a little coaxing, she volunteered to model for my class last year. Drawing the human body was what I was teaching at the time, and the nude you saw at the co-op was the result." His shoulders rose in a shrug. "She was in and out of my studio often since she was close by in Sarasota. End of story."

"I seriously doubt that's the end, Brant. You know a hell of a lot more about Suzanne than what you've told me."

Brant ambled slowly to a rack of canvases, stowed the painting in the rack and pointed to a grouping of chairs. "Have a seat, Paul. Can I pour you a coffee?"

"I'll sit, but no coffee, thanks."

Brant sat opposite Paul and placed his coffee mug on a stool between them. "First off, call me Rob, okay? I'm not the enemy here. I'm going to tell you what I know about her, and you can bank on it for the truth."

"That's what I'm after," Paul said, shifting forward in the chair, "the truth."

"I happen to think Suzanne Petrone is a very special person, not only in a sexual way. She is a beautiful woman, no question." Rob leaned forward, hands pressing on his knees. "I did try to hit on her. Christ, who wouldn't? But it didn't happen. She nixed it right away; said she was committed to someone, and only came here to while away some time, to see what my class was all about."

Rob paused, waiting for a reaction that didn't come. "Su-

zanne had some good suggestions for teaching the Impressionists. That seemed to be her favorite period. Hell, she could give
lectures on nineteenth-century American and French paintings.
She could be teaching art history in a college somewhere. I was
amazed that, being so young, she called herself a collector. You
probably know about that. Her trust fund?"

Fury was rising in his chest, but Paul fought it back. "Is that
why she was special to you, Brant?"

"Suzanne is special for many reasons. Because of her passion
for art, she has an understanding and an appreciation that few
others I know have. That's what attracted me in the first place.
She shared some of her knowledge of the Old Masters with the
students in my class, and she definitely added a dimension of
understanding for them. We clicked, Paul, on a professional
level."

Rob closed his eyes and drew a deep breath. "I was a friend
when she needed one, and I cared about her."

Paul sat back, wary, wanting to believe, but not believing
what he was hearing. The rub was that this guy knew more
about Suzanne than he did, and he was slick. Too slick.

"Suzanne called me last week from Sarasota. Said she trusted
me and needed my advice with a problem. The trust, she said,
went back to my relationship with her and the kids last year."
Brant looked away and Paul thought his eyes went soft. "What I
was doing for them, and the faith they had in me. At any rate,
she spilled her guts about her father and the gallery theft in
Maine. Said she thought maybe her father had someone following her here in Florida."

"Had someone following her? He's in prison. How could—"

"Petronelli was part of a powerful syndicate, here and abroad.
The Feds only got the tip of the iceberg in Florida when they
got him. If the Monet she presented to your gallery was identified in Sarasota as a forgery . . ." He shrugged. "Suzanne

claimed it must have been switched. Her father knew she had the painting before she came to Portland. He knew she brought it to New York from Paris, and he must have known she brought it to your gallery."

This was more than Paul expected to hear, more than he wanted to hear. *Why hadn't she contacted him?*

"Suzanne said at first she couldn't believe her father would mastermind something to incriminate her, but she's become more and more suspicious since the FBI interrogated her. She wants to go back to Maine, but she's afraid to leave Florida."

Paul swiped his fingers through his hair. "What did you tell her?"

"Told her to stay put. Do her usual Ringling thing and her gallery walks. I told her that I had a friend who could do some investigating, and he will know if she's being followed. I asked her to wait a week to contact me again. Meantime, I called Daniel. He told me about Rafferty bringing you down here."

"So you knew Daniel Kelly's plan all along?"

Rob nodded. "I was being cautious when you came in with Daniel. He referred to you as JP initially, but today when he said Portland, I knew who you were. Believe me, Daniel has been checking things out all week. Count on him. He knows what he's doing."

Chapter Sixteen

Molly said the spa would soothe his aching leg and he'd be glad for it. God knew he needed something to make him feel good after the session with Rob Brant. Paul sat at the edge of the heated pool, eyeing the Jacuzzi, trying to order things in his mind.

Daniel brought him back to Seaview and took off without a word. *There were perks because he was "family,"* Daniel told him. His uncle hired him to protect his property and assets in Boston and Florida. He would be free to take other cases, when time permitted, but Massachusetts was where he was licensed, and where Rafferty's influence was stronger.

His first investigation was the theft that happened the year they moved into Seaview, four years ago. Something was missing. If Daniel came to the States in his teens and was now in his thirties, what happened in the years before he became a PI? And what of Brant? Paul wanted to believe the guy, but . . .

Paul stared into the swirling water. He shook his head as though to shake away the questions boggling his mind. He inched his way into the steaming depth. No question that life in Florida was appealing. He sat on a low bench that curved around inside the spa, putting his head and shoulders just above water. Paul closed his eyes, lost track of time, and let the swirling water soothe.

Someone coughed nearby and he opened his eyes. Molly stood on the deck smiling, with a towel over her arm.

"I hoped you'd hear me, dearie. That leg will be healed in no time, but too long in there and you'll be a prune. Mr. R gets in the spa after his tennis matches, and I know the timing, so I'll leave this towel here an' you can come out now, if ya please."

My God, I think Tante *Margaret has been reincarnated here.*

Jacques Fontaine was not a man to feel sorry for himself. He spent his life building his career, his reputation, and his integrity. He would do most anything to defend his family or his career if threatened, yet he couldn't understand Paul's decision to go to Florida. The stolen painting didn't seem reason enough, because Paul was a guiltless victim, trying to do his job. The police and the authorities could surely solve the crime without his help. So why did he go?

Thinking about Paul's innocence clouded Jacques's thoughts about the surgery he was facing. Kathleen should be home in time for the surgery, and she probably wouldn't understand Paul's absence, either. He rocked in his porch chair, his thoughts as dark as the shoreline he could barely distinguish from the darkening sky.

The first rumblings of thunder joined a loud chorus of wind and waves, and brought Margaret to the open screen door. "Gonna be a storm, Jacques. You best come inside now so I can close this door."

He rose. Trying for a lighthearted response, he raised both hands in supplication. "What? You think I don't know enough to come in out of the rain?"

"No, no, *chéri.*" Margaret laughed. "I would never think that. I just wouldn't want you to have the experience I had last week when I was caught in that flooding rainstorm."

"I was teasing, Margaret, but I do remember that storm. It was the day you came home with a new hairdo, *n'est pa?*"

"*Oui.* But my Clare didn't want me to change my hair,

remember? Funny, eh, how young people make changes easily, but they expect you to stay the same." Margaret was quiet as they walked into the living room. She was thinking about Clare and Remi, but she couldn't voice her suspicions, not to Jacques, maybe not to anyone.

"Indeed, my dear, what you say is certainly true in my life. Maddy and Paul wanted me to remain their mother's husband. I know they resent Kathleen."

Margaret knew exactly how Paul felt about Kathleen, but of course she wouldn't comment on that, either. "Eh, *bien*. Time, *mon cherie*. Time mends. Tomorrow, I will spend early morning getting things prepared in the kitchen for the next few days, eh. Surgery is early Tuesday morning; now tell me again, when is Kathleen coming?"

"She's taking an American flight out of Chicago in the morning. It makes one stop in New York and arrives in Portland at three-sixteen tomorrow. Maddy will leave school early and pick her up."

"You know I would have been glad to do that, Jacques."

"I need you here, Margaret. I know you'll have everything ready, and I've told you about the fasting tomorrow, right? I have every confidence you and I can handle things as they come."

Margaret did a mental eye roll.

Molly not only spoiled Paul with little attentions after his soak in the spa, she didn't need much prodding to give him some skinny on Daniel.

"Mr. Rafferty put him through college, aye, and Daniel got a job with the Boston police. Daniel is a bright one. I was told he advanced to undercover investigator quickly, but that's the last I heard about that. *Himself* will probably tell you the rest," Molly said, "if you ask him."

When Daniel returned, Paul decided it was time to confront him about that and more. He tapped his finger on the list of contacts Remi gave him. "This detective from the Sarasota police. You've spoken to him?"

Daniel took a second look at Paul's list. "Aye, SPD crime division consulted with me when I provided intelligence for the prosecution in my uncle's burglary case. There's mutual respect and they trust me. That's how I was privy to the dealer who was approached with your missing painting. SPD was on him right away and checked him out with the FBI's district office. No prior convictions here, but the man moves around. Brant says he's from Italy."

"Have you actually talked with this dealer?"

"No. It wouldn't have accomplished anything. Rob Brant knew him. The man is probably one of a half dozen brokers and appraisers who buy and sell in the area. As far as Rob is concerned, if the dealer thought the painting was a forgery, it probably was a forgery." Daniel shrugged. "If you really want to check the man out, we can do that, but, I . . . I'd rather concentrate on your friend Suzanne. I've had her under surveillance since Rob called and alerted me that she *is* being tailed."

"Good Christ, man! Surveillance on top of surveillance?" Paul stood, turned his back on Daniel, and walked away from the patio table. His hands clenched and unclenched. "I've been following your lead, submitting to your *preliminaries,* and playing your game," he said in a voice edged with anger. He turned to face Daniel. "But I'm not a patient man. I've got a bigger stake in this than you know."

Daniel raised an eyebrow, but his eyes were flat, showing no emotion. He hesitated only a second. "I do know. I'm paid to know. We're going to change the pace tomorrow, but you've got to get control of yourself. Keep cool, or you'll blow it. I'll show you after supper what we'll be dealing with. We're going to the

Ringling Museum of Art. Suzanne has been going there on Mondays because it's usually a quiet day at Ringling, and I assume she must feel safe there. I'll brief you before we get inside, but you'll have to play it my way. Control, Paul. You'll need it. Control is the sharpest sword."

Margaret waited all evening for Paul to call. She had two calls from Clare. Each time Clare talked about Jacques's Sunday morning consult at the medical center and the mass that *Tante* went to without her, but Margaret made no comment. She wasn't naive; she had guessed what was probably going on at Remi's inn, but she refused to comment. Clare's conscience was her own problem.

Margaret had trials of her own. What would she say when Paul called? Maddy promised her father she would only call Paul in an emergency, but Margaret's promise was made to Paul.

Clare steered the conversation to Jacques's surgery. She had requested special duty at the medical center, to be with Jacques on Tuesday. "It's my last day off, *Tante*, but I'm glad I can be there for him."

"I'm glad too, *cherie*. It will be a comfort to your papa Jacques. Closing the door on yourself opens your heart to others, eh?"

Before Clare could respond, she heard a beeping on *Tante*'s phone. "That beep means someone is trying to call you, Mom. You must have call-waiting. Do you know what button to push?"

"No, and if Jacques Paul told me, I forgot. I'll just hang up now, Clare."

No sooner did she click the phone shut than it rang.

"Hi Auntie Mame, Paul here. I thought you didn't like cell phones, but I've called twice, and you were busy talking each time."

"It's my Clare. You shouldn't have given her my number. She still thinks I'm better than yellow pages."

"She's probably right. I suppose there's a lot to do when you're planning a wedding, huh?"

Margaret drew in a breath, pressing a thumb on her forehead with a little sign of the cross. *Mére de Dieu!* she wanted to say. "*Oui,* Jacques Paul. Things are moving along."

"Well, things aren't moving along the way I'd like down here, *Tante,* but we're taking a big step tomorrow. Maybe seeing my lady tomorrow . . . *comprenez-vous, Tante?*"

"*Oui. Je comprenes.* You be careful, hear?"

"I'll tell you about it tomorrow night when I call. In the meantime, how are you doin' with Pa?"

"I'm doing much better with his meals, but I may not be at Francois's Fancy much longer. Kathleen is coming home tomorrow." She heard Paul's intake of breath and his murmured "Oh, shit."

Margaret broke the pause that followed. "I don't have any details for you tonight, Jacques Paul. I just thought you would want to know, eh? *Bonsois, cheri.*"

CHAPTER SEVENTEEN

Walking at his side, Paul felt the silent stare of Daniel Kelly. He understood the first nod as they passed the Oceanus Fountain in the museum courtyard. Daniel lingered at the towering cast of David, and then would come the second nod. After that Paul would leave his side, climb the steps and enter the museum alone. Kelly didn't think any person following Suzanne would be inside the museum. More likely he would be on the grounds, watching and waiting, just as Daniel would be. Paul would meet Dan at the courtyard fountain right after he left the museum.

Paul hated the plan. He felt like he was playing a scene in a third-rate whodunit, but he objected to no avail.

"If you want the truth, you have to play it my way," Kelly said. "Desperate times call for desperate measures."

The new wing might be Suzanne's choice as it housed special exhibitions. But, first, Paul would stroll slowly through the galleries containing John Ringling's magnificent collection of sculptures and Old Masters, being constantly aware of other visitors to the museum, until, and if, he saw her. Last night's mental dress rehearsal came in the form of a virtual tour of the museum on Dan's laptop computer.

Amazing what was on the Internet. The same polished floors, ornate marble columns, burnished wood panels skirting painted walls; all was just as he saw it on the virtual tour video. The Italian-influenced galleries offered a magnificent background for the great Old Masters.

Paul wished he could stand before each treasure, just as the few people he observed were doing, self touring without a docent, but his eyes could focus only briefly on the paintings as he walked slowly through the galleries, watching visitors carefully. He was definitely not playing a third-rate scene; this place was a palace.

Benches, placed strategically for viewing paintings on either side of the long rooms, were empty until he entered what he thought was the Northern Italy Gallery. A woman occupied a center bench midway of the room. She faced a large painting on the right wall, the draped figure of a man.

Paul walked left until he was behind, yet adjacent to, the bench. He stared briefly at the muscle-rippled masculine figure in the painting, and then his gaze fell to the contour of the woman's profile, her eyes fixed on the painting. *Just like in Brant's sketch.* Long black hair fell across her cheek as she bent her head to write on a small pad in her lap. It was Suzanne.

Paul looked left and right. No one else was in the gallery, except for a docent sitting at the narrow far entrance. He moved forward to stand beside the bench.

She heard the footsteps and cast a sideways look. Her eyes widened, heightening a look of panic on her face. She quickly raised her eyes to the painting. "Oh, my God! What are you doing here?" she whispered.

She took his breath away. His stomach churned and his heart thumped. Never letting himself look away from the painting, he spoke each word slowly and carefully, pitching his voice so only she could hear. "I came to find you."

"You shouldn't have. You are in danger—"

"I'm aware of the danger."

Paul walked slowly forward to the painting, trying not to limp. He paused as though he were checking its inscription, then looked left and right again. He was at her side in seconds, pressing a scrap of paper into her lap. *Catholic church—five-minute walk from your hotel, twelve-thirty, tomorrow. Call RB for details.*

"We have to talk." Paul shot one desperate look at her before he walked away.

Outside, the fountain water shimmered in the bright sunlight, but it did nothing to lighten Paul's mood. He was visibly shaken.

Daniel appeared out of nowhere, removed his straw hat, and swiped a handkerchief over sweat glistening on his forehead. He nodded in Paul's direction and Paul began the long walk back to the car.

Maddy couldn't miss the flaming red hair and shapely figure of Kathleen being guided from the terminal gate by a middle-aged man.

"Madelaine, dear," Kathleen said as Maddy approached, "I'd like you to meet . . ." Kathleen looked up at the handsome man at her side, fluttered her eyelashes at him and obviously drew a blank.

"A fellow passenger from first class," the man finished for her. "Glad to have helped." He smiled as he handed an overnight case to Maddy. Releasing Kathleen's arm, he turned his back to her for a second. "I'm afraid your mother is not too steady," he whispered.

Quietly, not letting her feelings show, Maddy replied, "She's not my mother, but thank you. We'll manage."

Getting Kathleen through baggage and out to the car was *not* easily managed. Kathleen leaned heavily on Maddy's arm, blabbering on and on about how difficult it was to be around sick people. No sadness expressed for Jacques, only how difficult it was to come home to more health problems.

Maddy cast a sideways glance at Kathleen slumped in the passenger seat. *No sympathy for you; no sympathy whatsoever,* she thought. *I know she likes her wine, but I've never seen her drunk like this.* Relieved when Kathleen nodded off soon after they left the airport, Maddy was glad for the quiet. There had been no words out of Kathleen's mouth since Maddy reassured her that Jacques was really doing well *in Margaret's* care. *She's so smashed,* Maddy thought, *she probably couldn't even catch the inference.* Disgusted with Kathleen, but more worried about her father's reaction to his wife's condition, Maddy was hoping Margaret would be there to diffuse the situation when they arrived.

It wasn't necessary to alert Margaret. As they came through the kitchen door, the alcohol fumes were telltale enough. God bless *Tante* Margaret. Instantly, she poured Kathleen a cup of coffee and insisted she take the mug with her into the den where Jacques was waiting.

"You are tired from your long journey, eh, Kathleen? This fresh coffee will revive you. Madelaine and I will take your bags upstairs."

Maddy set the heavier bag just inside Jacques's bedroom. "I'm not going any farther, *Tante,* up here or downstairs. It was bad enough having to bring her here in that condition."

Margaret patted Maddy's shoulder. "I'm sorry it had to be you, Madelaine, but your papa thought it best I stay with him. Maybe Kathleen was drowning her sorrow, eh? That's what some people do, you know, when they want to escape. They drink."

"But do they always find a handsome shoulder to cry on?"

Margaret's puzzled frown prompted Maddy to bite her lip. "Forget that I said that. I'm just upset and anxious about how Papa will react. It's bad enough that he has Paul to worry about."

Margaret stopped in the hall outside Paul's bedroom. "You didn't tell Jacques Paul about the surgery, did you, Madelaine?"

Maddy looked mournfully at her brother's bedroom door. "No, but I wish he was here."

"Me, too," Margaret said. She took Maddy's arm to start down the stairs. "I must confess I did speak to your brother, only because I promised I would call him on that confounded cell phone he gave me. When he asked about your papa, I told him Kathleen was coming home, but I had no details."

Maddy stopped on the stairs and gave Margaret a hug. "What would we do without you, *Tante?*"

Paul walked the beach in front of Seaview, deliberately testing his leg in the sand. His mind was busy pondering every piece of information Daniel had given him when they lunched at the marina restaurant. The kinks in his brain were beginning to untwist. Daniel's briefing was the most detailed information he'd gotten so far. Maybe because he told Dan that the museum scene was the hardest thing he had ever done.

Dan said he knew where Suzanne stayed in Sarasota. It was a small residential hotel, turned into condos, a safe spot for downtown. She had stayed there a year ago for a few weeks of the season. Suzanne had been interrogated right after the painting showed up in Sarasota, but Daniel wasn't sure the Feds still had her under surveillance. Someone was tailing her, but he thought it was more likely her father's syndicate.

Jesus. Good Lord! This has become much too complicated. Maybe my pa was right. I couldn't have conjured up a more convoluted scenario if I tried.

Looking east, toward the road, he spied a cabana settled back in the dunes that seemed to mark the north end of Rafferty's property. He approached it cautiously and peeked inside. Two lounges filled the sheltered space, a small table separating them. Surprised that such a short walk caused his hip to ache, the lounges looked inviting. He could rest his leg, enjoy the view and watch the shore birds for a spell.

No sooner had Paul seated himself comfortably, than the

entrance to the cabana darkened with shadow. Hands on her broad hips, Molly O'Brien smiled down at him from under a big, floppy hat. She wore a flowered sundress as bright a blue as her eyes. "I thought you might be here, dearie. To be sure, it's a nice spot, don't you think?"

"Well, yes, it is. Is there a problem with my being out here, Molly?"

"No, no, 'course not. The Raffertys often sit here to catch the sea breeze. Aye, that's what it's for. I take a walk on the beach meself when Daniel's here. Gives us each a little space, you see."

That I can appreciate. "Is Dan still inside?"

"Oh, my, yes. He's on the phone. A call came from Mr. Brant while you two were at lunch in the city, and I forgot to give him the message. No disrespect intended, but Daniel can be irksome at times, when mistakes are made." Molly shoved her hands into the pockets of her dress and shook her head. "My fault though, so when Mr. Brant called back a second time, I thought I'd give himself some privacy."

Paul nodded. "Gotcha," was as far as he dared follow that thought.

"I'll be walkin' a little farther now, since I've done all me dinner preparations. You take your ease, dearie, and let me know if there is anything you need . . . anything at all."

Paul watched as she walked away. A pair of ibises pecking their curved red beaks into the water seemed to be following her. Sanderlings raced in a small flock, running so fast along the shore's edge it seemed they were running away from waves that rippled in. The birds were a good diversion, but Paul couldn't get Brant's call out of his mind. Did Suzanne need convincing to meet him tomorrow, he wondered? Was that why he's calling?

He left the cabana soon after Molly walked away, trying to hurry back to the house, but his hip resisted any speed but slow.

It was a painful reminder of why he was here and the mess he was in.

Daniel sat on the lanai, nursing a drink. "Will you have a scotch with me, Paul?" he asked, holding up his drink when Paul came in.

Paul shook his head. "I'm not sure I could handle whiskey right now."

"Ah, but ye might this one. Scotch is whiskey, but not all whiskey is scotch. This is my uncle's reserved Glenlivet. Smooth as silk."

"Okay, one then, but I'd like some answers with it." Paul sat opposite Daniel at an umbrella table. "What kind of questions did Suzanne have for your friend Rob Brant?"

Daniel poured scotch from a decanter, stirred in some ice cubes, and placed it in front of Paul. "You're better than an Irish setter, man. Right on point. Been talkin' to Molly, have you?"

"I met her on the beach, yes, and she mentioned the call from Brant."

"Rob Brant says Suzanne is scared about you're being here, Paul. Brant thinks it's pretty dicey you're going to meet her."

"And what do you say?"

"Rob may be right. You could be the reason she's being watched. Petronelli may still be pulling strings in Sarasota, looking out for his daughter. The man has powerful connections, no doubt about it." Dan sipped his drink, watching Paul. "Or it could be the syndicate has a long arm and wants you out of the picture. Either way, there's danger."

Paul took a healthy swig of his drink. "I sure as hell didn't plan on all this."

"Neither did my uncle. I called him, and he says it's time he called the bureau. Looks like you're still going to the church tomorrow, Paul, but you will have company. An agent will be calling with directions early in the morning."

CHAPTER EIGHTEEN

Margaret waited for Clare in the visitor lounge at the medical center. Never mind that Kathleen treated her like hired help, she thought; Jacques would want to see her. Hadn't he told Clare to make sure she got in to see him, rules or no?

Margaret had lit candles in the chapel, prayed the rosary and drove to the center as soon as Clare called. "The surgery went well," Clare told her. "Blockage was cleared with no complications. He's going to be fine. It wasn't just the surgeon's skills, you know. From your lips to God's ears, Papa Jacques always says. Your prayers are powerful, Mom." That made Margaret happy.

Her eyes brightened when the door swung open and Maddy, Patrick, and Clare came into the lounge.

Clare had the biggest smile of the group. "Everything went smoothly, Mom. Doc Halliday says he's confident that Papa Jacques will be giving him strokes as soon as the golf course opens."

"And what does your papa say, Madelaine? Is he awake enough to talk?" Margaret asked.

Maddy reached for her hand. "He's not only awake, but pretty alert. Papa asked for you, *Tante*. He told Kathleen that he wished to talk to you."

Margaret's eyes widened and she pushed back into the chair. "Uh-oh. Did that make a problem?"

Patrick and Clare both laughed at the same time. Clare

tugged her out of the chair. "Come on, *Tante*. Doc Halliday was Johnny-on-the-spot. He brought 'her nibs' down to the doctors' lounge for coffee. You're going to have alone time with Jacques."

Clare brought Margaret to Jacques's room, stopping at the door. "If I'm not back in ten minutes, come to the guest lounge when you're ready to leave. I'm going to grab some coffee and say good-bye to Maddy and Patrick."

Margaret opened the door and tiptoed in. Although Jacques was the only occupant in the room, the curtain between the beds was half drawn. She peeked around it. An EKG monitor blipped as lines moved across a screen. Jacques's eyes were closed. "Ah, *mon cherie*," she whispered, "I should come back later."

Jacques's eyes opened, and he raised a hand toward her. "I hear you, Margaret. Please stay. Can we talk for a minute?"

Margaret stepped closer, grasping his fingers in her hand. "*Certainment, mon ami.* Your surgery went well, Clare said."

"Yes, thank God, and you. I know you were praying, and I know Paul has been in your prayers, too. He is on my mind, Margaret. I think you are the best one to tell him about my surgery. I've told Kathleen you have a special arrangement with Paul to contact him in any emergency, and that I've asked you to wait until this ordeal was over with. It's not good for Paul to call the house and have Kathleen answer. She's likely to ask questions that he's not ready to answer. You know what I mean, Margaret. Will you call him for me?"

"*Oui*, I can do that, but I already told Paul that Kathleen is here. Nothing else, though, about you."

"Good. Then I'd like you to tell him the surgery was a sudden decision, everything went well, and I'm on the mend. That's not far from the truth, *mais oui?*" Jacques caught his breath on a sigh, and his eyes fluttered. "I'm still a little woozy, but please tell Paul I'll call him as soon as I get home, okay?"

Margaret patted his shoulder. "Not to worry, I will do that, but I think you must rest now, *chéri*. I'm going to send Clare back in now, okay?"

Jacques's eyes stayed closed while he whispered, "*Merci*, Margaret."

Margaret's mind whirled with all that was said before she left the medical center. Clare talked nonstop. First, would *Tante* go to the florist with her this week to help choose flowers for the wedding? Then as soon as Jacques was discharged from the hospital, Maddy would go with them to Portland to choose a wedding gown and maid-of-honor dress. "We're hoping Papa Jacques will be able to give me away," Clare said, "and, of course, we have to shop for a mother-of-the-bride dress for you, *Tante*."

Margaret kicked off her shoes and stretched out on the bed. *Never mind that Kathleen treats me like a glorified housekeeper. I am going to be mother of the bride!* She closed her eyes. *Mon Dieu, so much is happening.* The bell tone of her cell phone broke into her thoughts. She sat up quickly and retrieved it from the nightstand.

"Hi, Auntie Mame. You answered fast this time. Is everything okay?"

"*Oui*, Jacques Paul. That's because the phone is right beside me here in the guest room. I came upstairs to take a little rest, but I did intend to call you tonight."

"If it's not a good time, you can call me later, *Tante*."

"No, no, it's okay." Margaret felt caught between loyalties to father and son, but this was no time for hedging. "I have news for you. Your papa had some surgery today, on the arteries in his neck. I don't remember the name for it, but the good thing is he decided very quickly to have it done, and the surgery was successful. He asked me to let you know he's on the mend."

"Geez, *Tante!* These are the details you didn't have last time we spoke? You said Kathleen was coming home, but no information about Pa. Why didn't Maddy call me?"

"Because your papa didn't want to worry you, *mon cherie*. He said you had trouble enough down there in Florida. He doesn't want you trying to get a flight to hurry back here, so he asked us to wait."

"What about Kathleen? Did she come back because of my father, or because the old aunt died?"

Margaret was almost sure it was the former, but no one had actually told her. "I think she came home to be with your papa, but Kathleen and me, we are not too chummy, you know, so I don't ask questions."

"I'm with you on that one, *Tante*. So, Pa is okay and there's no other news up there?"

"*Oui*. . . . Oh, I almost forgot! My Clare is hoping your papa will be all better in time to give her away at the wedding. It's getting close, you know, and you will be home before that, won't you, Jacques Paul?"

"That's a question I wish I had the answer to. Things are getting complicated here."

Margaret lowered her voice, even though she knew no one was home. Being pledged to secrecy was beginning to weigh on her conscience. "Didn't you get to find Suzanne? You said you expected to."

"Yes, I did, but being with her is more dangerous than I expected. I can't go into details, but maybe after tomorrow I'll know more about the painting. If anyone asks about me, just tell them I'm working with Rafferty's private eye. Remember, mum's the word about Suzanne. In the meantime, take a break, Auntie Mame. Tell Pa I'm thinking of him and looking for a call as soon as he's home."

"I will do that, *oui*. *Bon nuit*, Jacques Paul."

★ ★ ★ ★ ★

His back stiff and rigid, Paul sat in the front pew staring at candles that flickered in the dim light of the sanctuary. Mass had ended. He had gone over and over the plan in his mind. It was a distraction unrelated to church as he knew it.

The bureau was specific, yet sparse with directions. "Attend the noon mass. Walk in like a regular parishioner, go to the front pew near the statue of Saint Joseph and stay seated when the mass is over. Suzanne has been told to go to the north transept when she enters the church, walk to the sanctuary and light a candle in front of the statue of Joseph. She should be able to see you when she turns away from the statue. She will enter your pew to kneel and pray.

"Check your surroundings before moving close enough to deliver your message. She will know that there is an undercover detective and a federal agent somewhere in the back or the vestibule. Stay constantly aware of persons around you."

Alerted to footsteps to his left, Paul's eyes followed the swirling skirt and swaying hips of a sylphlike figure approaching the candles. His eyes lifted to her black hair drawn back in a twist, fastened with ivory combs. He'd never seen her hair styled like that, but he knew it was Suzanne. She used a taper to light a candle, then turned abruptly to face him. A surplice-style white tunic revealed just enough of her deeply tanned neck and breast to make Paul squirm. He clutched his hands together tightly as she slid into the pew.

The wild desire in his heart to take her into his arms and pull her close was not going to be fulfilled. Paul checked the aisles and pews left and right of the altar. No one was in view.

Suzanne spoke first in a hushed voice. "Why the FBI? Why can't you simply come to my condo?"

Paul moved closer on the kneeler. "This was planned so they can nab whoever is following you. The car's been ID'd, but not the driver. It's crucial to locating the Monet. I *will* come to your condo shortly after you leave the church."

She rested her hips back against the pew, eyes down, twisting her hands together in front of her. Paul checked the area around them one more time. He leaned back against the pew and reached to cover her hands in one of his.

He couldn't let her know that his heart was pounding with fear, too. "Look at me," he said. They turned to one another and he found her eyes wet with tears that threatened to overflow. *Oh, God, I need control here.* "It's going to be all right, Suzanne. Trust me."

Suzanne nodded and rose, leaving Paul with concerns that pulled at his gut. He kneeled once more, this time with eyes squeezed shut in prayer. Minutes later, he opened his eyes to a shuffling sound. A sacristan was checking the altar linen and replacing flowers at the foot of the altar. Paul checked his watch. Time to get to the parking lot and find Daniel's car.

The blue Ford was one of a few cars left in the church lot. A Mozart sonata was playing softly when Paul opened the door. Daniel pointed to his iPod in the console. "One of the ways I drive away tension," he said, eyeing Paul. "You look wired, man. There was no action here in the lot. How did it go inside?"

Paul heaved an audible sigh. "Okay, I guess. Suzanne played her part, scared to death. She questioned the FBI involvement."

"It's the security of certainty. They have to be certain who's following her, and find out why. Anyone left in the church?"

"Two old women were all I counted."

"Good. We're on our way." Daniel started the car. "I'll idle near the front of the hotel to let you out and watch to be sure you get in. I've one stop to make and I'll be back at the entrance at two o'clock sharp. Watch your time. If you have a problem, you have my cell number."

Paul entered the brick building under a dark awning. He

pushed number 202 next to Petrone and picked up the phone.
"Yes."

"JP," he answered. A buzzing sound released the door which
opened to a corridor. Paul took an elevator to the second floor.

Suzanne opened the door as soon as Paul knocked. She
motioned him in and quickly locked the door. Track lights in a
narrow foyer caught the sleek darkness of her hair. She took
Paul's hand, leading him to a circular leather sofa in an
ultramodern living room.

As soon as they sat, she pressed a finger over his lips. "Just
listen, okay? I've got to get this out. It's what I wanted to tell
you when I came to Portland," she began, "but when I tried, I
just couldn't bring myself to do it."

Suzanne took a deep breath and clenched her hands in her
lap. "My father was a legitimate art dealer in Italy and here in
the States after he married my mother. It wasn't until I was a
teenager and my mom had died that he became involved in
what he called an *association*." Suzanne covered her mouth with
a trembling hand. Paul reached for her fingers and squeezed
them, holding her hand in both of his.

"My father taught me a lot about art, but being the naive,
trusting daughter, I thought his work was legitimate. I never
knew what he really was involved in until I started college. I
tried everything to disassociate then, but it was so hard."

Eyes brimming with tears, Suzanne spoke so softly, Paul
could barely hear. "My mother died when I was thirteen, and
he was all I had. I didn't want his dirty money, so I tried to
make it on my own until my mother's trust fund came to me.
That was in my last year of art school. I told you bits and pieces
about college, but I never wanted you to know the whole truth
about my father."

"You could have told me," Paul said. "I learned about it from
the news on TV. Then, all too suddenly, you took off for Florida,

and the shit hit the fan." Paul looked away for a heartbeat, then back at Suzanne. "The Monet was gone, and I ended up with a bullet in the hip."

A soft, moaning sound from Suzanne had Paul suddenly pulling her into his arms, holding her close. "I didn't mean it to sound like you made it happen. I never wanted to believe you were part of it but"—he held her out at arm's length and sought her eyes—"sweet Jesus, what was I to think?"

She silently shook her head. "I wasn't part of it. Please believe me."

He released her hands but not her eyes. "I came here to find the truth, Suzanne. When I got here, this guy, Rob Brant, tried to convince me about you. He knew things about your father that I didn't, but the biggest surprise was a painting. . . ." Paul shook his head, words failing him.

"I never thought posing would be a problem," she said. "The painting was for his class. That was all. I admired Rob Brant and thought I could trust him, but that was it, Paul. He befriended me when I needed help."

He felt her shy away. She pushed back into a corner of the sofa. He stared at her for several seconds. "Suzanne. Don't shut me out, now. Brant told me you wouldn't have sex with him because you were committed to someone. If that's—"

She closed the distance between them instantly, reached up to clasp his face in her hands and kissed him. It was fast and hard, but not without passion.

Paul shifted at the tightening in his groin. He knew there was little time left before Daniel's arrival.

"It's you, Paul. I don't want to shut you out. I wanted to fly right back to Portland the minute I heard about you, but I couldn't!"

"Oh, God, Suzanne. Rafferty's PI has got me following commands like a trained dog, and now the FBI is jerking my chain."

He pinched the bridge of his nose between his fingers. "I only have until two o'clock, and we haven't even talked about the painting. I need to know if it was switched for a forged copy."

"I think it had to be. The police said the dealer thought it was forged. The painting could show up on the black market, but I wouldn't know what to do—"

"Your father would know!" Paul suddenly pulled her close. "God, Suzanne, wasn't he selling forged copies of masterworks? That's what put him in Otisville prison."

Suzanne pushed back from his embrace. One look at the agony in her eyes, and Paul nudged her chin up to meet his gaze. He held her shoulders firmly in his hands. "I'm sorry. You didn't need that reminder. Please. Just tell me what you think."

"What I *know*, not what I think, is that the Monet I brought to Portland was authentic! It was on loan to me from a collector in Paris. He agreed it could be exhibited short-term, and I brought it home and presented it to you at Cornerstone. If a forgery showed up, then it had to be switched, and that had to be the syndicate working its evil machinations. I just can't believe my father was behind it."

Paul's eyes blazed. "But you left me, and you didn't come back. Why?"

"Okay, you want the truth, here's the truth. Before I came to Portland, I visited my father at the prison. He told me that this apartment in Sarasota was bought and paid for by my mother's legacy, and I should use it or rent it out, because he sure as hell couldn't anymore."

"So you've been here before?"

"Yes, but not often, because it was one more tie to my father. My mother was a wealthy woman who had many ties to Sarasota. Her philanthropic efforts with the arts were how my parents met. What was hers was his, and that's how he got this apartment. A large part of her estate was put in trust for me. I became quite wealthy at twenty-one. I couldn't tell you all this then, so I made it look like I was coming to Florida on a little vacation."

"Then why didn't you come back to me after the break-in?"

"I didn't learn about it *or* the shooting until the FBI came to interrogate me when the painting showed up in Sarasota. The federal agents are the reason I'm still here. I was ordered not to leave."

The house phone gave two short rings, punctuating her words and startling them. Paul looked at his watch. *Not even close to two o'clock.*

Suzanne walked quickly to the phone in the kitchen. When she returned, her face was pale. "That was the Sarasota police. They're on their way up."

Paul stood beside Suzanne at the door while two plainclothes policemen showed their IDs. The gray-haired, raspy-voiced one spoke. "Detectives Canfield and Maroney. Sarasota CID. You are Suzanne Petrone?"

"Yes," Suzanne said, warily. "What is this about?"

"Can we step in for a moment?"

Suzanne nodded and Paul stepped aside as the two walked from the foyer into the apartment. Both men looked around the living room, and the younger of the two pointed toward a hall leading to the bedroom. "You live alone here, Ms. Petrone?"

"Yes," Suzanne replied, her cheeks reddening as she shot a glance at Paul.

The old guy towered over Paul. He was tall and slim with close-cropped gray hair and sharp, dark eyes beneath bushy brows. Dressed in a dark, rumpled suit, with a loosened tie, he reminded Paul of Columbo—except for his height.

Aside from his appearance, it was the name he gave that caught Paul's attention. *Canfield was one of the names on Remi's contact list.* Paul stepped toward the detective. "Detective Canfield, my name is Paul Fontaine and I—"

The younger cop interrupted, "We know who you are, Fontaine."

"Hold on, Maroney." After a frosty glance Maroney's way, Detective Canfield's voice gave away his authority. The younger officer was obviously a new partner, maybe a rookie. Canfield cocked his head to look down at Paul. "You done good at the church, Mr. Fontaine, so listen up now, and we'll have time to talk later." The man had a disconcerting, down-home attitude and a lazy southern drawl that didn't seem to fit the badge or the title.

Canfield moved closer to Suzanne. "Miss Petrone, we're working with a federal agent from the Art Theft Program. We've apprehended a suspect, and we'd like you to come down to headquarters to see if you can identify him."

CHAPTER NINETEEN

The ride to headquarters in an unmarked car was short and not as frightening as it had loomed in Suzanne's mind before they left the apartment. Detective Canfield assured her she was not being arrested, but her cooperation was vital to the case. Although Suzanne was the one requested, Canfield made it clear that Paul should come along because Daniel Kelly would be at the station to meet him. *Sure as hell, Daniel will be where the action is.*

"How long have you known Kelly?" the detective asked Paul.

"Not long. A few days," Paul replied.

"You hire him?"

"No. He works for his uncle."

"That'd be Counselor Sean Rafferty, owner of Cornerstone Gallery?"

Paul nodded, surprised and unsure where the conversation was going.

"Mr. Rafferty send ya'll down here?"

Paul shrugged. "He had a part in it, yes." *Not the time to reveal more than that. This guy probably knows everybody on Remi's list.*

Detective Canfield turned to Suzanne. "So, the missing painting links you two together. Is that right, Ms. Petrone?"

Suzanne nodded with pursed lips.

"Well, we can take our time getting down to the department. It takes a while to establish a lineup, ya see." He shot a sideways glance at Paul. "Even with the best of connections." The detective raised an eyebrow at his partner. "You ready for a nice *slow* drive, Maroney?"

The observation room at CID was just like the ones Paul had seen on TV cop shows. Daniel waited at the door, nodded to Canfield and guided Paul past the glass wall, down a hall into a small conference room, leaving Suzanne with the detective.

Six men were lined up behind the glass. They were similar in appearance, mostly looking like tourists, or casually dressed Floridians, all male, all white. Suzanne struggled with her emotions. She looked at each one carefully. Then, turning to Detective Canfield, she pointed to the second man in the lineup.

He was stocky, with massive shoulders and muscles bulging beneath the short sleeves of a guayabera shirt. A neatly trimmed salt-and-pepper mustache matched what was left of straggly gray-and-black hair that barely covered his balding head. A faded scar stretched from his left eyebrow to his ear lobe.

"That one. Number two. He looks like a man my parents hired. Nicholas. Nickie, my dad called him. When I was younger Nickie was a driver for my mother here in Sarasota, and since then he did odd jobs for my father in New York and Florida. Kind of a courier, I guess."

Suzanne looked up at the detective, shrugged, shaking her head, then looked through the glass once more. "It's been so long since I've seen him, I can't be sure, but if that's Nickie . . ." Suzanne looked away, chewing at her lip. "I remember my mother being very kind to him. He lost his wife and child in a train accident. He was one of a few survivors." She tapped a finger on her cheek, looking up at Canfield with eyes that held sadness and fear. "The scar is what I remember most."

"That's good enough, Ms. Petrone. I think we're done here. Come along with me now." Detective Canfield ushered Suzanne past the observation room, into the small conference room at the end of the hall.

The detective nodded to Daniel, who sat closest to a woman sitting at the only table in the room. Paul sat stiffly in a straight chair at the opposite side of the room. "Ms. Petrone, this is Agent Richards from the Federal Art Theft Team."

Agent Richards could have been a model, except she wasn't dressed in the latest fashion. She wore the "in-power" costume of FBI, a dark-blue suit with a crisp white shirt, open to reveal just enough full breast to tempt. Long-legged, she was almost as tall as the detective. Agent Richards stood, extending a hand. Her pasted-on smile was wasted on Suzanne.

"Ms. Petrone has a keen eye, Agent Richards," Canfield said. He tapped his finger on the single file lying on the table. "Nicholas Makopulous, Florida resident, private cabbie, originally from Manhattan. That's New York, hear? A middle-aged widower, he moved to Florida permanently last year. SPD ran his name through files, and he's pretty clean. Has a laundry list of traffic fines, but other than that, he's likely telling the truth about the surveillance. I believe it's a match."

Detective Canfield turned to Suzanne. "Makopulous told us he was hired by an attorney to keep an eye on you, Miss Petrone. To see that no harm comes to you."

"An attorney? What attorney?" Suzanne asked.

"The office is following up on that right now. If you want to press charges, we'll be holding Makopulous, waiting for the attorney who hired him to come forward and corroborate his story."

Suzanne shook her head and met his gaze. "I couldn't press charges." She kept her eyes on Detective Canfield for several seconds. It seemed she gained strength from him, for suddenly she turned and squared her shoulders. She stepped close and leaning forward, spread her hands on the table and glared at Agent Richards.

"When I was questioned initially by the bureau, I was told to stay in Sarasota. I assumed agents were keeping an eye on me. Instead, I learn it was someone else trying to protect me. I've been given no information about the progress of your investigation, yet it was a painting on loan to *me* that was stolen. I do want that painting found, but I also want my life back. I want to leave this city. Now!"

The heavy silence was broken by a knock at the door. All heads turned.

Out of the corner of his eye, Paul saw Agent Richards give a nod to Daniel when Detective Canfield disappeared into the hall. Daniel rose, motioning with his head to Paul. "Step outside for a moment, Mr. Fontaine."

Paul reluctantly followed Daniel out the door.

Detective Maroney stood a few feet away with Canfield. Paul heard the last of his words. "The attorney in question is waiting with Makopolous down the hall."

Daniel huddled with Paul. "Good timing," he said. You and I need to move along, now."

Paul shot him an incredulous look. "What? She's in there with a barracuda. The answer to the surveillance question is out here, and you want to leave?" Paul balked, shaking his head. "No way! I've got to know Suzanne is going to be okay."

Detective Canfield stepped close. "Everything under control here, Daniel?" He didn't wait for an answer. He clapped Paul's shoulder, leaning close between the two men, his husky voice deliberate and in command. "The counselor in question is from a law firm representing Ms. Petrone's father. She'll be relieved to know that, and I'll be taking her back to her condo as soon as we're through with the lawyer." He gave a two-fingered military salute in the air. "Stay in touch, Kelly." Canfield turned on his heel and headed back to the conference room.

The message was clear. They were finished here at headquarters. Paul reluctantly agreed to go to lunch after Daniel reminded him they hadn't eaten since early morning.

So preoccupied with all that had happened at the church and at headquarters, Paul didn't pay much attention to where they were until Daniel parked the car in Bayshore Park. They walked through a fancy arched sign toward Marina Jacks Restaurant. "It's hard to take this in, Daniel," Paul said.

"What do you mean?"

"I mean how *you* fit in here with these guys, even with the icy bitch from Washington. You all play the same game, except for Canfield. He seems different."

Daniel snorted. "He's southern charm different. Detective Canfield's a subtle pro with twenty years' experience in homicide before he came into special investigations. I've never met his match. I got lucky on my uncle's robbery case. Most of these guys were watching, including Canfield, and it was my ticket back into their circle. Agent Richards . . ." He raised his eyebrows up and down. "She's a specialist from the highly trained Art Crime Team, and that's a story for another day."

The conversation ended when they entered the waterside restaurant and, at Daniel's request, a hostess took them upstairs. It was late enough that the lunch crowd had pretty much left, so she seated them at a window table. When Daniel bent forward to sit down, his sport coat hung open just enough to reveal a .38 revolver in a body holster. It was the first time Paul noticed that he wore a gun.

A waitress was at their table in seconds. Paul waited until Daniel ordered two scotches, and the waitress left. "Do you always carry a gun?" he asked in a low voice.

A muscle in Daniel's cheek twitched and he adjusted his coat. "Mainly when I come into the city, but not to worry. This place is a safe spot. No trouble here, just the usual boaters coming in for a quick lunch, or the elite crowd coming upstairs for dinner. I like to be where you get a good view of the bay. Can't resist the water. How about you, Paul?"

Paul nodded. "Ayuh. I was brought up on the Atlantic and I guess it's in my blood. At least sailing is."

Daniel took the intricately folded white linen napkin out of his wine glass. "First-class place, aye?"

"And you were used to that in Boston, right?"

"Oh, you're quick," Daniel said. "Parry and riposte. But me, not always first class, no." Daniel looked down at the boats in the marina. "My last duty with BPD was undercover at the docks in Boston. It was no first class."

"Molly told me you worked undercover in the crime division. That how you got so savvy with all this procedural crap?"

"Molly?" Daniel cocked his head, shaking his head and sharing a rare smile. "She's right. There was learnin' on the job, aye."

He picked up the menu, seemingly deep in thought. Paul suspected he wasn't thinking about what to order. The waitress brought their drinks, repeated the specials for the day, and Daniel ordered the grilled fresh tuna. "You'll like it, trust me." Paul nodded, holding up two fingers. The waitress smiled. "Good choice," she said, leaving with the order.

Daniel took a long pull on his drink. Seemingly lost in his thoughts. A twitch of sorrow crossed his face. He swiped at his mustache and stared again at the boats in the bay. "It ended badly in Boston. Long story short, my partner was killed in a drug bust, a shoot-out in the harbor. I was put on leave, under suspicion during a follow-up department investigation." His steady gaze stopped for a second. He looked away and cleared his throat.

"I was cleared, but it ruined my head for police work in the city. I resigned, and when this opportunity came up from my uncle, I took it."

"You didn't stray far from the field. Any regrets?"

"No." Daniel leaned back in his chair, extending a hand to the Gulf beyond the window. "There are no regrets in paradise."

CHAPTER TWENTY

It was almost five-thirty when Daniel and Paul arrived back at Seaview. Molly was waiting in the kitchen with her notepad in hand. "You've had two calls Daniel, and one was from *himself*." She tapped her pad with a pencil. "I wouldn't be waitin' long to return that one." She raised an eyebrow and cocked her head at him. "You hear?"

"And the other call?"

"That was from this number." She pointed to her paper, tore the sheet from her pad and handed it to Daniel. "He said call that number at seven this evening. The gentleman had a raspy southern drawl, sounded real polite, but he didn't give a name."

"Thanks, Molly."

Paul watched as Daniel headed to his room. "Guess I'm not so popular, huh, Molly?"

"Not true, lovey. Wait." Molly's mouth twitched and broke into a big smile when she looked at her notepad. "You got a call from a woman. She said to call Margaret when you get a chance."

"In that case, I won't wait to return that one either." Paul retreated to the guest room, fearful that Margaret might have bad news.

He sat on the edge of the bed, clicked his cell on and hit Margaret's number. "*Tante*, it's Paul. How did you get Rafferty's number here? I thought we were using cell phones."

"It was easy to get Mr. Rafferty's number from Sister Agatha,

142

and I did use my cell phone, at noon today, and again at two. You didn't answer, Jacques Paul."

Noon today. *Oh, God. Twelve-o'clock mass.* "Oops, I'm sorry, *Tante.* I turned my cell off in church, and I guess I forgot to put it back on."

"In church! Oooh, *bon, chéri.* On a weekday too!"

Anxious to change the subject, Paul reached for a pad and pencil from the nightstand. "Is Pa worse? If I should call the hospital, I need the phone number, *Tante.*"

"No, no, Jacque is not worse. He will be coming home tomorrow. Your papa is not the problem. It's Kathleen. She's making things difficult here."

"I'm relieved about Pa, but Kathleen—now that doesn't surprise me. When has she ever been easy?"

"Madelaine thinks that it's a drinking problem. Since she came back from Chicago it's been a bad scene."

"*Tante,* I'm sure you know that a drinking problem doesn't happen in two weeks' time. She must have had the problem long before she went to Chicago. She always did like her wine, and maybe Pa's been hiding something from us."

"Well, it's out in the open now as far as we can tell, and your sister doesn't know what to do. The latest hurt is that Kathleen's looking to fly back to Chicago this weekend if Jacques is recovering okay. Of course, she expects me to stay and help."

"Damned if that doesn't sound just like her. I know her excuse is the aunt who was supposed to be at death's door, but the old gal is sure taking her time dying. She's probably rich, and Kathleen wants a piece of it. Either that, or she's just using the aunt as an excuse."

"Jacques Paul, Kathleen is your papa's wife. Whatever you think about her reasons cannot help Jacques now. He is too proud to talk about his problems, and certainly not now, anyway."

143

"How about Maddy? Pa always seems to listen to her."

"A problem shared is a problem halved, Jacques Paul, and your sister thinks you should be here. That is why I am calling, *comprenez vous?*"

Paul swallowed hard. "What does the doctor say about Pa?"

"The doctor says he must avoid driving and physical activities for several weeks."

"Weeks! Geesh, Auntie Mame. Would you be able to stay with him at least until I get back?"

"When will that be?"

"I *think* things are wrapping up here. Maybe by this time next week I'll be home."

"But what about the painting? You haven't told me a thing about that. And Suzanne. Is she still supposed to be a secret?"

"The painting is still missing, *Tante*, but the FBI has a lead they're working on. Suzanne . . ." The picture of her standing up to Agent Richards flashed in his mind. "Maybe it's time Suzanne shouldn't be a secret anymore. Tell Maddy I'll call her later tonight, and hang tight about Kathleen, for now anyway."

A fax came into FBI Tampa Field Office from Interpol. An American suspect was apprehended in Milan, Italy, with a painting. Agent Richards divulged the information while Paul and Daniel waited for Suzanne to view the lineup. Agent Richards made it clear to Daniel that she and another ACT agent were immediately assigned by Bureau Command to Milan. They would be working with Interpol and the foreign service legal team. Most likely they would extradite the suspect. Richards was waiting on travel arrangements.

The woman personified cold, calculating confidence: a bitchy dame, Paul thought. More, he wondered how Suzanne would react when Agent Richards told her the details. Paul had seen the sparks between them when Suzanne had taken a stand.

Hopefully, Detective Canfield diffused the situation. Maybe they'd let up on Suzanne now. Maybe it was time both of them got the hell out of Florida.

Paul sat on the lanai watching the setting sun ride behind clouds. A quick rain shower had cooled the air, sweeping the beach clean. Daniel's footsteps made a path in the wet sand as he walked toward the house. Daniel rarely walked the beach. He used his red hair and fair complexion as reason to avoid Florida's sun, but at twilight, that couldn't be the reason. Paul suspected it was a cell-phone call he made to Detective Canfield.

Daniel left his sandy sneakers at the door. "A fickle evening," he said, coming to sit opposite Paul, "but I predict it's about to get better for you, Paul."

"How's that?"

"The number Canfield gave me to call was actually your lady's cell phone." Daniel took the scrap of paper from his pocket and handed it to Paul. "The division worked out an alteration of the original surveillance plan for Miss Petrone."

"You mean the Feds are backing off watching her now that their field of operation has changed?"

"Let's just say there's been a compromise. You can call Suzanne, and she'll be free to meet with you until or unless either of you are threatened."

"Threatened!" Paul's eyes blazed. A wave of anger swept over him. "What kind of bullshit is this? I came here at risk in the first place. You knew that, and Rafferty knew that, too."

"Exactly. Granted, there could be an attempt on your life if the perps think you're muddying their attempts to fence the paintings. CID will watch both of you for a little longer. When there's no longer a threat, you can go back to Portland, and Suzanne will be free to leave Florida."

"And you think this deal is better for me! I feel like the bait in a rat trap. I don't give a rat's ass about CID, but I was beginning to think you were human, Kelly."

Daniel pursed his lips and shook his head. "Don't kill the messenger, Paul. If the greedy bastards who stole the painting can pull off a double sale, they'll stop at nothing to do it. My job is to protect the boss's interests and yours."

Paul stood, staring at the phone number on the paper. "Sorry, man, but I still can't believe Suzanne would go along with this."

"Not her choice, then, is it?" Daniel said.

Chapter Twenty-One

Paul left the lanai without another word to Daniel, his thoughts in turmoil. What could he say to him anyway? *He's an ex-cop who's trying to walk the line between the Feds, his uncle, and the local crime division. Seems sincere enough, but the guy is one strange PI. I've never even heard him curse.*

He followed Daniel's footsteps down the beach, scenes playing over and over in his mind: Suzanne's fear at the Ringling Museum, the uncanny tryst in the church, and the scenario in her apartment. Counterbalance that with Suzanne's gutsy courage in standing up to Agent Richards at headquarters. How could she possibly go along with this hell-fired scheme? Hadn't she had enough, too?

Paul looked up at the darkening sky. Incredible ribbons of color gilded dark clouds, creating an afterglow worthy of a canvas. *Pleine air, pleine air* assailed his mind, but his body was canceling the message. Paul's hip ached from the pull of walking in soft sand. It had hardly bothered him today in the city, but there had been little time to notice. Maybe the nightly soaks in Rafferty's Jacuzzi were helping. That spa might be his only pleasant memory about this island.

He sighed with relief when the cabana loomed ahead. He had to hear Suzanne's side of the story. Seconds before he reached the cabana, his cell phone rang. Puzzled, he looked at the small screen. It was Maddy, and he hardly got the phone to his ear before she spoke.

147

"Paul, I'm not waiting any longer for *Tante* Margaret to relay messages from you to Dad to me. The surgery is over, and I need to make myself clear about things here. Are you ready to listen?"

"Well, hello to you, sis. Yeah, sure, I'm listening."

"Sorry, Paul, but this can't wait. It's about Kathleen. Maybe *Tante* Margaret told you that she arrived drunk. Well, for the past forty-eight hours she hasn't really sobered up. She pretends, you know, when she's at Dad's bedside, but he's still under medication, so he probably doesn't notice. Either that or he won't let on, but I think it's got to be hurting him."

"Have you tried to talk to Pa about it?"

"Patrick thinks it's a personal matter between them, and I should stay out of it. So, no, I haven't. Yet."

"Patrick's got a point. It *is* Pa's business, but unfortunately everybody gets affected. *Tante* told me she's been under fire from Kathleen, too. 'Course, *Tante* doesn't feel it's her place to talk to Pa either."

"Come home, won't you, Paul? Kathleen seems to be less troublesome when you're around. Together maybe we could make things a little easier for Dad. I know he worries about you, and that's definitely not good for him."

Paul wasn't prepared for this. He'd intended to make a call to Maddy after he called Suzanne and decided what to do. There was no easy way to explain about Suzanne and the reasons he couldn't leave Sarasota. Not in a phone call, anyway.

"I wish I could say yes, but it won't be possible for me to leave here for a couple more days, Mad. It's too complicated to explain over the phone, but there are serious reasons. Maybe you could talk to *Tante*. She understands."

"I've tried, but she clams up when I ask her why it's so important for you to be in Florida."

"Tell her I said it's time to share the promise now."

"And what does that mean? This is no time for games, Paul."

"Games! Uh-uh. This is not games. No Trivial Pursuit down here, believe me. I'll be home soon as I can. Count on it."

"I guess I don't have much choice in the matter, huh?"

"Right now, neither do I, babe."

Destiny is not a matter of chance; it is a matter of choice. Paul remembered the line from a speech an actor made. The actor and the film were long forgotten, but the line had stayed with him. It was the same message the nuns taught him. *God allows us to choose our destiny.* Suzanne surprised him by echoing that very sentiment when he called and asked her if she was safe.

"Yes. Detective Canfield stayed with me, and we talked for a long while. He convinced me that my choice to come to Sarasota was the decision that sealed my fate. I was fulfilling my father's intentions to save me from any connection to the theft in Portland."

"You mean Canfield really believes your father wasn't in on the theft or the switch?"

"I'm pretty sure he sees it that way. He said his division is working on that angle. My father may have known about the break-in, but he couldn't have been involved with it, or he would never have sent me to Sarasota and had Nickie watch me. It had to be the syndicate."

Paul was in turmoil. "I'm not convinced, Suzanne. If the real Monet shows up in Milan, then where is the forged painting?"

"All I can tell you is that the men my father was dealing with have been working black-market deals in the States for a long time. They must have access to forgeries and places to fence them, but an authentic Monet—that could bring millions more on the foreign market."

"That may be so, but it feels to me like CID is setting a trap right here, and I'm not ready to be a victim, Suzanne. I want to get the hell out."

There was a long silence. "You will have protection as long as you're with me, Paul." He could hear her sigh. "I was afraid for you when you came to Sarasota to find me. I'm still afraid, but I want to be with you. I think you know that now." Her voice cracked. "And I don't want it to end this way."

"It's not going to end."

"Then, come here tomorrow, Paul. I need you."

Margaret's dream came back. The second one this week. She was sitting at a table in front of a painting. The painting looked to be about two feet wide, she guessed, as her extended hands came toward the canvas in a mental measure. A tall, uniformed man sat opposite her watching. He was foreign-looking, his uniform nothing like that of an American police officer, yet she felt strongly he was a policeman.

As Margaret's fingers lightly touched the edges of the canvas, the man leaned forward, drawing her attention to him. His eyes flared, glinting fiercely. His head gave an almost imperceptible shake.

Margaret stared into his dark eyes, then moved to his mouth and his exaggerated handlebar mustache. She clutched her hands together in her lap and lowered her eyes to the painting. Red sailboats in blue water. Green stuff floated on the surface of the water. Maybe lily pads? Two figures stood on the shore. A lady held an old-fashioned umbrella. The picture was an oil painting; that much she was sure of.

Suddenly, she sensed someone's presence, but when she looked around, no one else was in the room. Margaret breathed deeply and listened. A woman's voice murmured, *"Mais oui, bateaux rouges sur le Seine."* Margaret's eyes darted again around the room, but there was no woman. Only the man with the big mustache, his mouth stretching wide in a clown-like grin. He clapped his hands together, making a loud sound, and Margaret woke with a start, sweating in tangled bed sheets.

"*Mon Dieu!* Twice, this dream. The same man, the same voice, the same painting. I have to call Jacques Paul," she thought, "first thing in the morning."

Sunrise had zero chance to bathe Casey Key in light, but Paul wasn't aware of that until he stepped outside his bedroom glass doors into the dark. He walked toward the next property and looked eastward over the tall shrubs that separated Seaview from the house next door. He was hoping to watch the sunrise, but ominous thunderheads scudded over rooftops on the bay side of the road. A flash of lightning revealed rocking sailboat masts in the chop. Paul ducked back inside and headed for the kitchen as rain blew in from the Gulf.

Molly had warned, last night, that the weather forecast was not good. She was at the kitchen island, chopping green peppers and ham for an omelet. A small TV built into the cabinet wall was tuned to the weather channel. "A tropical cyclone affecting the southwestern Caribbean was upgraded to a tropical storm. The no-name storm gained strength and speed as it moved away from the Cayman Islands. Western Cuba is bracing for seventy-five-mile-an-hour winds."

The TV announcer was petite and pretty like Paul's sister Madelaine, but that wasn't the only thing reminding Paul of Maddy. The forecast brought to mind the hurricane that had once sent Maddy traveling through time.

"Hurricane season doesn't start until June, does it?" Paul asked.

"No, but June is on our heels, dearie. Next Monday, in fact. I'm making a hearty breakfast for the two of you, and after you've eaten, Daniel will be taking me shopping up to the Publix in Nokomis. We take these forecasts seriously, and I'll be stockin' up for the weekend just in case the tropical storm comes our way."

"Were you ever here during a hurricane, Molly?"

"Indeed, we all were. 'Course, I mean the Raffertys, Daniel and me. We had only been here in the house two months when Charley came roarin' up the coast in two thousand four. Evacuated we were, eh, Daniel?"

Daniel had come into the kitchen, slid onto a stool at the counter and nodded his head at Molly. "All the barrier islands were evacuated, Paul. The eye wall struck Punta Gorda and Port Charlotte. Those harbors are just south of here."

"Was there much damage here on the Key?"

Daniel shook his head. "No. Some pool cage screens and roof tiles, some flooding, but no structural damage here. Most houses are on pilings. Boats bayside took a beating, though. Ripping winds and pounding rain, aye. That's when Uncle put a new roof on." Daniel cocked his head toward the TV. "Ever been in a hurricane?" he asked.

Paul nodded. "One came up the northeast coast in September a couple of years ago. Our home is right on the shore, and the roof took a little damage, same as here." *And life wasn't quite the same after Maddy disappeared in the storm.* . . . "I wasn't there, but I came home and helped clean up afterward."

Molly set full plates in front of them and poured coffee. She turned to face the TV screen with hands on hips, listening. The announcer was wrapping up her report. "The no-name storm is expected to reach western Cuba by mid-morning."

Molly shook her head as she stared at the map on the screen. "For the love of all that's holy. That's the path that Charley took! Hurricane Charley was bad news for southwest Florida, and if the storm turns this way again, we're in trouble." She took off her apron, grabbed her pad and headed for her room. "I'm goin' to get ready, Daniel."

As they ate breakfast, Daniel explained the preparations necessary if a hurricane watch was declared. "Motorized hurricane shutters will be activated across the entire front of the house and on Molly's and my bedroom windows, which face east. Lanai furniture will be transferred to the garage. A storm surge could bury us anyway on this narrow island, but we'd be evacuated long before that could happen."

When they finished breakfast, Daniel brought their dishes to the sink. "Keep the weather channel on, Paul, and we'll be back in an hour or so."

Paul looked out at the beach. Wind-driven rain was pelting the pool cage. "How about Sarasota? You said you'd take me this afternoon."

Daniel sighed. "They'll have the same weather. Are you sure you want to go today?"

"Hell, yes. A tropical storm is a piece of cake compared to the muddle my life is in right now."

A call from *Tante* Margaret, describing her dream, was a ray of light penetrating Paul's dark mood. He could hardly believe it. *Tante*'s description of the painting was dead on! *Red boats on the River Seine*—Monet's masterpiece is exactly that! She even described the only distinct figures in the painting. Margaret couldn't have known anything about the painting until her dream. She had never even seen it!

Paul told *Tante* she might have answered a very big question about the missing painting. *Tante*'s dream, like a vision, yielded thoughts and perceptions that placed the Monet in a foreign city. It could be considered a clue like the one she provided in Remi's investigation. As far as Paul was concerned it was a big piece of the puzzle. Logic and intuition arranged the pieces until they fit.

Daniel might believe it, but if Paul's word wasn't good

enough, he could ask his uncle to check Margaret out with the nuns at the Retreat House. She was a shoe-in there.

At last the roulette wheel was spinning in his direction. The spin could stop on the money if only he could convince Suzanne and Detective Canfield that a clairvoyant had found the real Monet before the Feds did.

Chapter Twenty-Two

Relentless rain up and down the sun coast kept the cautious indoors, but Paul was determined to put an end to his time in Sarasota. He convinced Daniel that Margaret's dream *could* be his bargaining chip with Detective Canfield. Daniel listened to Paul relate Margaret's dream, not once, but twice before they left Seaview. In the end, Paul's persistence won out. Daniel packed rain gear into the car and they headed for Sarasota.

Wind-driven rain blowing across the windshield made for slow going as the two drove north on Tamiani Trail.

"Margaret is the person who called on my cell phone the first day you took me to Sarasota," Paul said. "Remember? She's the aunt who was taking care of my father, but isn't really my aunt."

"I remember you said the woman is a psychic who refuses to use her skills for hire."

"That's right, she *is* a reluctant clairvoyant, but I think she's reluctant because of her faith. Margaret is a devout Catholic and years ago the nuns at a private girls' school told her it was not natural to foresee the future. Her psychic skills have only been used to help family during a crisis. 'Course, the Fontaines *are* family to *Tante* Margaret."

"But how could she be a credible witness?" Daniel argued. "Canfield can't count on a dream from a psychic living a thousand miles from here."

"Do you think your uncle would believe it?"

"What? Look Paul, my uncle must have thought it was worth

bringing you down here to Florida, but bringing you back to Portland before either painting is found—that is, *if* there are two paintings—makes no sense."

"Well, it makes sense to me. Margaret Chamberlaine could be a credible witness." Paul paused before he delivered what he thought was his ace in the hole. "She has ties to a favorite charity of your uncle." Paul glanced sideways to see if that made an impression. He caught a raised eyebrow.

"There's a retreat center that used to be a girls' school I just told you about. Margaret went to that school, and I believe your cousin, Sean Rafferty's daughter, was once a student there. *Tante* Margaret still has a good relationship with the nuns who taught her. They're the same sisters who now run the retreat center."

"Are you talkin' about Star of the Sea Center?"

Paul's eyes widened. He nodded. "You know about the place?"

"Aye, I know about it because I drove for Uncle when he made a visit to Biddeford Pool. He gave an endowment to the retreat center in memory of my cousin."

"Well, I only brought it up in case your uncle needs to verify Margaret's integrity. He could call on the nuns up there. They all know her."

Daniel shook his head. "Fontaine, you're an opportunist."

"Persistent is a better word, Daniel. I need every chance I can get."

Added to the strain of driving in a torrential downpour, Daniel's patience with Paul was wearing thin. "Well, you can save your words for Detective Canfield. He knows my uncle, but he may want to know more about your family. Tell him about your place up there on the shore at Biddeford Pool, your sister the school teacher, and this psychic who is not your real aunt."

"Sweet Christ, is there anything you don't know about me?"

"Aye, there is, but it'll have to wait. The windshield wipers are hardly fast enough, and I need to concentrate to get you to the dance on time."

A stream of taillights blinked in the murk as traffic slowed to a near standstill at the intersection of SR 301. Cars were slowly turning west on the trail, and Daniel made a quick decision to take 301 straight up to Ringling Boulevard.

Earlier, Daniel had called and told Detective Canfield to expect them between two and three. It was well after three o'clock when they arrived at SPD headquarters. Upstairs, the division offices were quiet compared to the front desk in the squad room when they arrived. Daniel said so as they entered the small office where Detective Canfield waited.

"Yep. Phones've been ringing off the hook down there," Canfield said. "Endless fender benders, and stalled cars. Beats me why people are out in weather like this."

Paul shot a suspicious look at Daniel, and Canfield caught it. "There's a staff lounge next floor down where you can get coffee, Daniel," the detective said. "Maroney just went down. You want to wait there or join us now?"

"Coffee sounds good. I'll be back."

Paul didn't like the feeling he was getting, but he wasted no time after Daniel left. He told Detective Canfield about Margaret's dream and his own gut feelings that the original painting was now in foreign hands, not in Sarasota. "In my opinion a forged copy may have been brought to Sarasota to muddy the trail, while the real thing was transported overseas. I think the dream proves my theory."

Canfield raised an eyebrow. "Your theory," he said, pursing his lips and shifting in his chair. He continued to stare at Paul, but said nothing.

Paul added some backstory about Margaret. "In the state's Marine Patrol investigation of an unidentified drowning victim last year, Margaret Chamberlaine was able to name the Jane Doe by using evidence from the body. She also marked the place where the victim lived. Her testimony was a crucial lead in the case."

"And the perpetrator—she ID him, too?"

"No. The case got complicated. It became a double murder with drugs involved. Maine State Police and the Feds got involved." Paul waited, but got no response from Canfield. *If there was ever a time to use Remi's list, this is it.* "State Lieutenant Frank Meloche was the chief investigator."

Paul thought Canfield's eyes held a momentary flash of recognition when he named Meloche. The detective scribbled something on a desk pad, and then he paused, his dark eyes fixed on Paul. His fingers drummed on the desk.

Meeting the detective's gaze, Paul waited. *Maybe I've scored some points.*

"Fontaine, my man, suppose you tell me the real reason you had Kelly drive you here in a storm that's predicted to become the first hurricane of the season. Most of our concerned citizens would batten down at home and brace for the storm, especially out on the Keys."

Paul was dumbstruck. *What the hell? I thought the dream spelled it out.*

"The real reason? I believe in Margaret Chamberlaine. Whether she's in Maine or here makes no difference to me. She knew nothing previously about the missing Monet. All she knew was that a painting was stolen, yet she described it perfectly. From what she told me, I believe the authentic painting is in a foreign country, and as far as I'm concerned I'm out of danger in Sarasota. The danger isn't here if the authentic painting isn't here. I came here today to tell you that and to tell Suzanne. As you put it, Detective, when you came to Suzanne's apartment, the missing painting links Suzanne and me together."

"True. It does, but with FBI involved, procedures are not that simple. Your interpretation or theory?" He shrugged. "All in good time, Fontaine, it will play out. Meantime, the surveillance is—"

Paul stood and placed one hand out, stop-sign flat. "The surveillance be damned. You can't hold me here—" Before he could finish, Daniel opened the door.

Detective Canfield stood and nodded at Daniel. "I think we're done here, for now, Kelly. "Did Maroney update you about the hotel parking lot?"

"He did."

"Take care and stay safe out there. We may be in for a big one."

Paul waited to explode until they entered the elevator. "Christ Almighty," he said in a tight-lipped voice, his anger bouncing off the walls. "He didn't say shit about the dream! When I spelled out my theory about no painting here, no danger here, all he said was 'All in good time.' Well, I haven't got good time. I'm needed back in Maine."

"Did you tell him that?"

"No."

"Maybe you should have started with that. You gave your theory to top-floor brass and expected him to suspend surveillance immediately?"

"He wasn't really communicating with me. Seems you were the only one getting directions." They had reached the lower level, approaching the exit. "What the hell is this business about the hotel parking lot?"

"Wait till we're out of here and I'll explain," Daniel said. The wind and rain had worsened. The hooded slickers Daniel brought helped a little as they stepped out into the downpour, but sloshing across the flooded lot to the car soaked their shoes. As soon as they got in the car, Daniel threw back his hood and mopped his face with a towel. He patted down his mustache and tossed the towel to Paul.

"This trip was not a good idea, Fontaine. Updated forecast has the tropical storm headed into the Gulf with sixty-mile-per-hour winds. Molly's probably scared silly by now, with good reason."

Paul didn't want to hear it. "The hotel parking lot. What about it? Was Canfield talking about Suzanne's building?"

"Yes. The hotel apartment building has an entrance in a side parking lot. When I brought you to see her, you went in by the front entrance on the street. She's been told to only use the side entrance from now on. That goes for you too, if you were to see her, but it's a moot question now. One of Canfield's men is stationed in that lot watching who comes and goes, but she's goin' nowhere today, you ken? Her watchdog won't be there either. Called off an hour ago for a storm alert."

"Perfect. Who needs him anyway? I'll make the visit short, okay?"

"No. It's not a good idea."

Paul pounded his fist against the door. "You mean Canfield doesn't want me there."

"*He* didn't say that. 'Twas his partner filled me in on the orders for the day. I'm givin' you my gut feeling, Paul. This storm has frigged everything up and we should be heading back to the Key. Now."

"No way. We're only blocks away, and I want to see her now!" Paul knew he was acting like a spoiled kid, but he couldn't seem to get control. Nothing was working as he'd hoped, and now the storm was jeopardizing everything.

Daniel adjusted dials to clear the fogged windshield. The wipers beat a staccato tattoo as the engine started, but the exit sign to the street was barely visible. Wind battered the small car as it swung away from headquarters, shaking it like a maraca.

Paul's sideways glance at Daniel's white-knuckled grip on the wheel triggered a twinge of regret. Daniel steered slowly through deep water in the street. Before they reached the first intersection, the headlights picked out a car ahead swerving off the road, barely missing a stalled car blocking its path.

Daniel pumped the brakes and passed the stalled vehicle, water spiraling and spraying from the wheels. "That does it," he said. "I'm not taking you to Park Hotel, Paul. This is stupid. I gave you her cell-phone number last night, so call her. Call your *inamorata* and explain."

Paul's heart and head did battle for several seconds. He pulled out his cell phone and dialed, listened to it ring five, six times with no answer. He punched in the number a second time and waited. No voice mail, no answer. Nothing.

Paul choked down panic as the headlights picked up the intersection of SR 301. Daniel turned south at the intersection. "Wait! We can't go back to the Key yet. Suzanne's not answering her phone. Something must be wrong. Jesus, stop the car, Dan!"

Deliberately, Daniel put his turn signal on. He pushed his right hand out toward Paul as you would a child to keep him firmly seated. Then he slowly eased the car into a parking space in front of a Seven-Eleven. Daniel whipped his cell phone from his belt and clicked on a preset number for SPD.

"The division will have to handle this one, Paul. No way in hell are you goin' in there cold."

CHAPTER TWENTY-THREE

Canfield immediately dispatched a squad car to Park Hotel Apartments when Daniel called him. Waiting for a response from SPD during the nightmarish drive back to the Key was harrowing enough, but nothing was as stunning as the actual call that came twenty agonizing minutes later.

Rain beat down on the hood of Daniel's car and hammered against the windshield. Their headlights picked out the sign for Blackburn Point when Detective Canfield's gravelly voice crackled over Daniel's speaker phone. "Dispatch called in a break-in at number 202 Park Hotel Apartments. Lone occupant"—static—"Miss Petrone, attacked and drugged"—pause—static—"possible robbery."

Paul's hands knotted into fists. "God!" he screamed at the voice. "Is she all right? Was she—"

"EMS is transporting the victim to emergency at Doctors Hospital"—more crackling and static—"CSU is on the way. Stay alert and available on this line, Daniel. Signal is breaking up, but when I have more, you'll have it."

"Will do," Daniel answered. The click-clack, swish-swish of the windshield wipers was the only sound after a loud click from the speaker phone. They were approaching Seaview on Casey Key Road. Daniel cast a quick look at wind-whipped whitecaps in the bay, then at Paul's anguished face. "No blame on your shoulders, man. Or mine."

★ ★ ★ ★ ★

They could see that Molly had moved all the furniture from the lanai to the garage and activated the hurricane shutters. She rattled off some Gaelic words when they entered the kitchen, but such was her obvious relief to see them, she wiped tears from her eyes at the same time. "God be praised yer home," she said. "I put tea on as soon as I heard you pulling into the garage, Daniel. It must have been terrible driving."

"The worst. But you should have waited to lug all the furniture."

"It was the storm movin' so fast. It became a named storm as it moved over water in the Florida Straits. The TV images showed it heading north-by-northwest with fifty-mile-an-hour winds after you left, Daniel. When it became a hurricane watch, I was worried sick about you two."

"Aye, I knew you'd be, but we're here now, and only a little the worse for it." He jerked his head toward Paul and handed her the wet coats. "Thanks, Molly. You can give him the tea. Myself, I'll be needin' a hot shower and some quiet time." Daniel headed for his room.

Paul slipped out of his wet shoes and walked zombie-like to the nearest chair in the living room. He sat, head in hands, staring ahead but not really seeing the wide-screen TV in front of him.

Minutes later Molly stood over him holding a steaming mug. "Here's a little whiskey and honey in hot tea, dearie. You'll have no Jacuzzi now with the hurricane shutters drawn, and more's the pity for your leg."

Paul reached for the mug. "Thanks, Molly, but it's not my leg bothering me, it's my head. Tension I guess, because I don't usually get headaches."

"Maybe the light bothers you? We turn on all the lamps.

Otherwise it's gloomy as a cave in here when the shutters are drawn."

"No," Paul said, rising a little unsteadily with his mug of tea. "I don't think it's the light. I think I'll take this into the bedroom and stretch out for a while."

Molly patted his shoulder. "The toddy will help, God willing. It'll chase the drearies and damps away *a mhuirnin.*"

Paul closed his eyes at what he thought was another of her Irish endearments. "Thanks, Molly. If things change with the forecast, or anyone calls for Daniel or me, will you let me know right away?"

"That I'll do. I'm sure Daniel must be resting now, too."

Paul turned off all lamps in the bedroom. A small night-light by the bathroom door shed just enough light by which to strip off his damp clothes. He drank the tea and lay down between cool sheets, welcoming the darkness. The hurricane shutters muffled the roar of the wind and the sea. He turned from one side to the other.

Chase away the drearies and damps? It's a friggin nightmare! Headlights, pounding rain, howling wind and Canfield's emotionless face spiraled through his mind. *The victim is being transported. . . . Who would want to harm her and how did they get in?* The panic in the car and his helpless guilt played over and over. Eventually, physical and mental exhaustion triumphed, and sleep took over.

The elevator ride seemed endless, but there she was, opening the door. Her welcoming smile turns to shock. She backs away and runs through the living room, screaming. A hooded, black-clothed figure moves swiftly after her. Her locked bedroom door caves from a crashing blow, and a gloved hand sends it banging against a wall. The specter pins her struggling body down on the bed and an eerie wail pierces the air. Drawers are flung open and closet shelves emptied. A lamp crashes to the floor, its intact bulb spraying an arc of light on the rubber boots of a shadowy hulk beside the bed.

A knocking sound came softly at first, then louder and sharp, like the pain in his head. Paul blinked and bolted upright, trying to focus on the small triangle spreading from the nightlight. A muffled voice behind the door called, "Telephone for you. I have the phone here. Are you okay in there?"

"Oh, Lord!" He wound a sheet around himself and fumbled his way to the door. It opened to a sliver of light and Molly's frowning face. She thrust a cell phone through the narrow space. "It's your lady friend. Okay, Paul?"

Lady friend? He stared at the phone, recognizing it as his own cell phone. "Yes, okay. Just trying to wake up." Still staring at the phone, he remembered that he and Daniel handed over their wet raincoats and shoes in the kitchen when they arrived. The cell was in his slicker pocket, at the ready, while they drove back to the Key. Molly must have taken it out. Paul mumbled his thanks and closed the door.

"Hallo, hallo. Are you there, Jacques Paul? What's happening? I've been holding on this phone forever."

"Sorry, *Tante.* Sorry for the wait. I just had a terrible nightmare, and I'm in a kind of crisis here." Paul sank down against the pillows.

"I think I know the reason, *mon cher.* Maddy says there's a hurricane forecast where you are and the lines to Florida have been so busy she hasn't been able to reach you."

Paul looked at his watch. "Maddy's half right, but the storm isn't the only problem. Have you told Maddy about Suzanne, yet?"

"*Oui,* but not all the details about Suzanne's papa. Just enough so she understands why you went to Florida."

"Well, all hell broke loose this afternoon. Suzanne's apartment was broken into, and I couldn't get to her because of the storm."

"*Sacre bleu! Un voleur?*"

"Yeah, it looked like a robbery, but nothing was stolen and she ended up in the hospital. We had to return to the Key without seeing her."

"Is she hurt bad? Does the break-in have to do with the painting?"

"The painting? Yes, it's most likely connected, but I don't know yet about Suzanne's injuries. This storm has everything bollixed up."

"Did you tell Suzanne about my dream?"

"Not yet, *Tante,* but the police were told." *Damn. This is not where I want to go right now.* "How about Pa? Is Kathleen hanging in with him?"

"Your papa is better since he's home. He will call you soon, *mon chéri.* I had a long talk with Kathleen. She is going back to Chicago, but not just yet. I'll wait till you come home to tell you all about it, okay?"

Puzzled, but relieved, Paul said, "Okay, *Tante,* but meantime, tell Maddy I'm safe and I'll call her as soon as I can. Give my love to Pa."

"*Oui.* Both of us keep you in our prayers, Jacques Paul."

"Thanks, Auntie Mame. I need them."

Paul had slept less than an hour before *Tante's* call came, but the sleep helped to clear his mind of one worry. Things were relatively sane back home. He showered and changed before coming out to the living room. Something smelled good in the kitchen, but Molly wasn't there.

He walked into the living room and began pacing back and forth in front of the television, not wanting to watch news releases about the storm that had thwarted his plans. He paused now and then to focus on details in the room, things that up until now he'd paid little notice to. One long wall was mostly a media center: a fifty-two-inch TV at its center, a DVD player and racks of DVDs flanked the left side. Surround sound piped the weather forecaster's voice to every corner and probably beyond the lanai, but Paul tuned it out, silently cursing the hurricane.

He spotted a beautiful seashell, a perfect Scotch Bonnet nestled on its stand, between a pair of silver framed photographs.

The posed family in one picture gave Paul his first glimpse of Sean Rafferty. The man stood in front of a gated courtyard, an imposing figure with snow-white hair and the same blue eyes as Daniel. His arms were linked with a smiling young woman and a thin, lanky young man. It had to be Daniel. A shock of red hair and freckled face, sans mustache, dated the photo maybe fifteen years ago. Paul picked up the picture and stared so intently at the faces, he wasn't aware of movement in the room until Daniel stood beside him. Paul immediately put the photo back and searched Daniel's face. "He called?" Paul asked.

Daniel shook his head silently.

Paul started to turn away. Daniel's hand on his shoulder was an obvious staying force. He pointed to the framed picture Paul had just put back on the shelf. "Do you recognize him? Uncle hasn't changed all that much. A few wrinkles and a slight paunch. He ages well. I can't say the same for myself."

"That is you, then. Is the young woman Sean's daughter?"

"Aye, that's Emily. Sweet and soft she was, very much like her mother, the gentle lady in the other photo. I was very fond of Emily. Someday I'm going to have Brant copy the two likenesses together, me and Emily. He's good at portraits." Daniel didn't think about what he'd said until the words were out, and he saw Paul's frown. "Oops, Paul. I didn't mean anything by that." He turned his gaze to the kitchen. "I can smell stew cooking, and Molly must be in her room. You hungry?"

Paul shook his head. "I've got a wicked headache."

"Food will help. Your head probably aches because you haven't eaten. I'll see if she's ready," he said, shuffling in his slippers up the hall to Molly's room.

Paul stood in front of the TV. A map showed the storm tracking northwest in the Gulf. The weatherman announced, "Tropical Storm Sybil's winds have strengthened to seventy miles per hour, just short of a hurricane one category." The forecaster's pointer followed the arrows on the screen. "Tracking northwest in the Gulf, it should make landfall in less than twenty-four hours. The good news for folks in the Sarasota–Tampa Bay area is that Virgil is heading west toward Alabama and Mississippi."

Paul heard a muted ring tone and voices coming from Molly's room. Molly emerged, hurrying down the hall.

"Oh, my, and you're up and waiting, too?" she said when she saw Paul. "Since you were both resting, I took a little nap myself. Never heard a thing till Daniel came knocking," Molly bustled into the kitchen. "The stew won't be worse for it, though. Nice and slow it's been cookin', and it'll be ever so tender. I'll have it on the table in a jiffy."

No sooner had she spoken than the lights flickered and the house went dark and silent.

"Oh, my, now!" Molly called out. "Paul, you're not to worry, hear? Stay where you are, and I'll have a hurricane lamp lit in a minute."

Molly was a gem. In minutes she set a small glowing lamp on a table near Paul. She lit tall candles on the dining table. "All prepared we are for emergencies," she said. "Daniel knows where to set the switch for the generator, and we'll have power with that, too, if it doesn't come back on by itself."

Minutes later, Daniel walked down the dark hall toward Paul, sober faced. Taking Paul's arm and moving with him toward the far end of the living room, he spoke in a low voice. "Canfield just called. Suzanne has no serious injuries." He paused for a minute to let that sink in. "She was injected with a powerful drug, which kept her unconscious for quite a while."

Paul opened his mouth to speak, but Daniel held up a hand like a stop sign. He frowned and shook his head. "God knows why. A large dose of the drug can cause respiratory arrest." Daniel placed a hand on Paul's shoulder. "But she is rallying, and she's been moved to a private room for monitoring overnight."

Paul's face left no doubt of his anguish. "If someone was clever enough to get into her apartment, then the hospital—"

"Her room is guarded. The CS unit found no incriminating evidence in the apartment. The place had minor damage, the usual burglary mess, tables overturned, closets rifled, a painting ripped off the wall, but no prints. Multiple prints on the lobby enterphone were sent to the bureau for identification. All we can do is check with the hospital in the morning."

Chapter Twenty-Four

Molly called them to dinner. The power flickered on as they sat down, went off again, and this time it stayed off. "Thank God for candles, but I think we'll need the generator later to finish up in the kitchen," Molly said.

Paul had to force himself to eat. Questions in his mind begged for answers. *Why was she drugged? If the person was masked like in my dream, then she couldn't have known her assailant, so why did she let him in? Who in God's name was it, and what was he looking for?*

Molly nattered on about the hurricane. "I'm thanking the good Lord we're escaping the brunt of the storm. The people along Alabama and Mississippi shores are probably being evacuated as we speak."

"I don't see how it could go from a tropical storm to an almost category-one hurricane and make landfall in less than forty-eight hours. It doesn't seem possible," Paul said.

Daniel passed the bread basket to Paul. "It's not unprecedented," he said. "There was a storm last year that developed from a weak low into landfall in less than twenty-four hours. We're just lucky that this one tracked northwest in the Gulf."

"If the power comes back, maybe by morning we can open the shutters and see what things look like. What do you say, Daniel?" Molly asked.

"Maybe. I don't want to use the generator for too long at a time tonight, just enough to keep the things in the freezer from spoiling. We'll listen to the portable radio and see what directives the county emergency manager has given. Power outages can be more widespread than we know."

"Will there be problems getting off the Key?" Paul asked.

"There's always a problem getting off barrier islands. Without power, the swing bridge closes the north route, but if we had to evacuate, we would go to the south end of the Key and get on SR 41 from there. This one came up so fast, and with Molly here alone, I hadn't begun to think about evacuation. The few year-rounders on the Key are probably still here, anyway. Not everyone leaves when they are supposed to."

Two hurricane lamps on the coffee table spread soft light around their chairs, and the night held a little less tension. Maybe it was the scotch Paul and Daniel sipped after Molly went in for the night. Daniel's portable radio was set to a classical FM station.

Paul felt bereft of family and friends. No one to confide in. He closed his eyes, listening to the music. Why had he ever agreed to come here? He struggled with the answer his heart knew better than his head. Daniel seemed to understand him, and although Paul was still irked by Daniel's foreign mannered machinations, he sensed his concern tonight. He wanted to trust him.

"Tell me what you think about the break-in? Do you think it was a random burglary?" he asked.

Daniel shook his head slowly. "No, not random, but I do think there's a connection to the painting."

"But why search her place for the painting? It doesn't make sense. And why was she drugged?"

"Motive. It's got to be all about motive, and a better mind than mine will ferret out the reason." Daniel checked his watch, rose and picked up the portable radio from the table. "Remember my stress eliminator?"

Paul nodded as Daniel gestured to the music coming from the radio.

"I'm going in to lie down with Mozart. This is his Serenade in G—*Eine kleine Nachtmusik.*"

Paul cocked his head, a puzzled frown creasing his brow.

"The composition is called 'A Little Night Music.' Appropriate, aye? There's a caveat, Paul. Research has shown Mozart's music provides spatial temporary reasoning. In other words, Mozart makes you smarter." Daniel smiled as he lifted one of the lamps to walk away from the small circle of light. "It does work."

He stopped a second later and turned back to Paul. "Maybe I'll set my alarm to turning on the generator in a few hours. That is if Florida power and light doesn't oblige us first. In the meantime, help yourself to the Glenlivet. It may help you sleep."

This guy has to be the weirdest PI in the world. Always in control, never curses, and now Mozart! Lifting the decanter of scotch brought a vivid image of Jacques and the worry about whether Jacques was really going to be okay. It also brought the realization that Paul needed to speak to his sister. A call to her was long overdue. By her calm, discerning demeanor, Maddy often diffused desperate situations. Paul punched her number on his cell phone.

Maddy sat in her father's kitchen at Biddeford Pool. *Tante* Margaret poured tea before taking a seat beside her at the table. "So, did your brother tell you about his *amoreux?*"

Maddy's mouth twisted into a tight smile to hear the French word for sweetheart, but her eyes quickly became sad. "Yes, but it certainly wasn't a happy tale. I understand now why he agreed to go to Florida, and why he was hesitant to tell us about Suzanne."

Tante Margaret sipped her tea. "*Oui.* Jacques Paul is a proud man, but more to his credit, he didn't want to bring scandal to the family. Especially now, to your papa."

"From what Paul said, he doesn't understand why she continues to be in danger . . . why the break-in? It's a tangled web that doesn't seem to have a solution."

"Did Jacques Paul tell you about my dream?"

"Yes, and I'm sure it has meaning, but Paul didn't think the police were very impressed. I am, though, *Tante*, and I also want to hear about you and Kathleen. How did you ever get her to admit she has a problem?"

Margaret shrugged. "By listening, I guess. When two share a burden it gets lighter, *mais oui? Mon Dieux*, but your stepmother was carrying a lot of baggage! Kathleen talked on and on about her first husband, how she always wanted children but was barren, about his early death that she couldn't cope with. She had a breakdown, you know." Margaret reached for Maddy's hand, and her gaze never faltered. "She told me that her father was an alcoholic, and she thinks she has inherited his genes."

"So if she thinks she has a problem, what about Papa? Did she talk about him?"

Margaret nodded. "That was the sad part. She said her desire to drink gets worse in every crisis, but Jacques doesn't see her drinking as a problem."

"And you believe her?"

"Madelaine. A hand that is always open or a hand that is always closed is a crippled hand. I think Kathleen's hand has been closed for a long time, so I opened mine to her. I believed her, *oui*, and I advised her to speak openly to Jacques about all that she told me." Margaret raised a hand, forefinger pointing for emphasis. "Then I told her she should seek help."

"Did she agree?"

Margaret paused, eyes wide beneath raised brows. "*Oui*, she did both! Doc Halliday set her up with a rehab in Chicago, and your papa seems content to see her go."

"Oh, *Tante,* forgive my doubting mind, but you achieved something neither Paul nor I would attempt. I don't know what this family would do without you."

Margaret smiled and refilled their teacups. "Convince my Clare, eh? She thinks I meddle."

"Uh-uh, never, *Tante.* Clare's world is topsy-turvy now, with the wedding less than two weeks away. I'll make it clear to her that you are definitely not meddling."

CHAPTER TWENTY-FIVE

Tropical Storm Virgil's winds lessened considerably overnight, but in the early hours of morning the beach at low tide looked ravished. Palm fronds, branches and debris littered as far as you could see on the north key. Luckily, neither Rafferty's nor the neighboring properties showed major wind damage, but remnant rainfall was still heavy and the narrow road was flooding. The bad weather would make for slow driving, but Paul felt grateful that Daniel made no objection to taking him to the hospital.

He listened to Daniel's music during most of the trip up Interstate 75 to Sarasota. Neither had much to say until they reached the exit for the hospital.

"I'm not sure if Canfield will be there," Daniel said. "I know he has a uniform outside her door."

"You mean a cop?"

"Yes, and he's been advised we're on our way." Daniel drove west at the Bee Ridge exit and a right turn at the next intersection brought him in sight of the green-roofed hospital. He found an empty parking space near the entrance, and they hurried from the car into the main entrance of a complex of pink sand-colored buildings.

Paul ran a hand through his hair. He watched Daniel's calm, in-control expression while his own jaw muscles worked and his feet shifted one to the other on the elevator ride to the third floor.

Just as expected, a policeman sat outside room 328. Daniel showed his ID, and the cop nodded.

As soon as the door opened, Daniel's "in control" expression changed to surprise. It was the investigator's first up-close-and-personal view of Suzanne. Her beauty was more astounding than Brant's painting. Even with the oxygen tubes in her nostrils, her ivory porcelain features, ebony hair and deep-set hazel eyes were a breathtaking sight. Daniel remained standing inside the door while Paul went to her bedside.

Suzanne's eyes blinked rapidly and filled with tears. "I don't understand," she said, her voice small in the sterile room.

Paul reached for her hand, but she pulled it away. "Is he another agent?" she said pointing toward Daniel.

"No. This is Daniel Kelly, a private investigator. He represents Mr. Rafferty, the owner of the gallery. I'm staying with Daniel at the Rafferty home on Casey Key."

Daniel nodded to Suzanne. "Miss Petrone." He tapped his watch with one finger and shot a warning look to Paul. "Mind the time, aye? Doctor's orders from Canfield. I'll be outside with the officer." Daniel pushed the door open and disappeared as it swung shut.

Paul captured her hand this time and studied her tenderly. He sat on the edge of the bed and gently stroked stray hairs away from her face. "I forgot that we had orders to keep this visit short." His eyes closed for a second while his head shook slowly. "If I could only have come to you yesterday, maybe none of this would have happened. I did try to call you. Were you told about that?"

She nodded silently.

"I cursed Canfield mentally and tried desperately to persuade Daniel, but there was no way I could get to you in the storm."

They stared at each other for what seemed a long time before Suzanne spoke. "Detective Canfield told me that the police found me after you alerted them. First thing this morning an agent questioned me but I told them *only* what I remembered most . . . opening the door and running, screaming, into my bedroom. Then the jabbing pain in my arm."

Suzanne looked away for moment. She was trembling when she turned to fix her gaze on Paul. Her voice quavered. "There was one thing that I refused to talk to them about. I . . . I hedged, Paul. On purpose." Tears that had threatened now trickled down her cheeks. "When I answered the entry-phone call, I was sure the muffled voice said 'JP.' Maybe it was what I wanted to hear, but that's the way it sounded to me, and that's why I let him in. I didn't dare tell the detectives about that until I told you."

Paul's face was a mix of shock and confusion. "JP? My God, Suzanne!"

Suzanne pointed to the door. "The man you're with? Does he call you JP?"

Paul shook his head. "Not since the day I arrived. It couldn't be Daniel. He was driving me from the precinct when I called you. We met with Canfield, then the storm caused such havoc on the roads that Daniel insisted we go back to Casey Key."

"Could he have arranged the break-in and—"

"No. Definitely not. Daniel works *with* the police. Canfield told us you had a guard protecting the entrance to your building, so we thought you were protected. At Daniel's urging, I called you to let you know I couldn't get to you."

Suzanne sank back against her pillows. "I was trying to protect you by not telling them about the entry phone. I didn't suspect you, Paul."

"Being in Daniel's car is all the vindication I need. I don't think the police would suspect me, but they sure as hell better find out who used my name to get in."

"Oh, Paul." She raised her arms to him and he held her

tenderly. She buried her face in his chest. "There's more, and I'm not sure I can handle it."

Paul raised her head to cup her face in his hands. Ever so gently, he kissed her forehead and her eyes, then grasped her hands in his. "Whatever it is, I'm here for you, okay?"

Her voice caught on a sigh. "This will be hard, Paul. A federal agent is communicating with the prison warden. My father was told about the break-in and my hospitalization. It's part of a scheme, supposedly, to help us both. The FBI will arrange a conference call to him at the prison, and they want me to talk to him about the attack and the danger I'm in. Detective Canfield's convinced that if my father thinks I'm being hurt, he will cooperate. He will give them a name."

"Can you do it?"

She closed her eyes, and the agony that crossed her face spoke louder than her words. She nodded, slowly. "I have to try."

The door opened suddenly and a nurse set the kick stand to keep it open. Paul stood, and the nurse moved briskly to Suzanne's other side. "Doctor is coming in to check you for discharge, Miss Petrone."

Paul's head swiveled toward the open door just as Daniel's head and thumb moved in synch to signal him out. *Damn. Every minute with her is timed, and it's never my time.* He managed to ignore the nurse's inquisitive glance, squeeze Suzanne's fingers and whisper, "I'll wait."

Tante Margaret drove the short distance from Francois's Fancy to Star of the Sea Retreat House. *Sorrow always comes in threes,* she thought. *First Paul, then Jacques, now Remi's papa, Jamie. Mary Windspirit cherished visiting with their daughter, but the trip to North Carolina took its toll on Jamie. It was back to the oncologist for more testing, and wait.*

Remi and Clare are cautiously waiting, hoping Jamie's cancer has not advanced.

Jacques is waiting to see if Kathleen's rehabilitation prevails.

Paul is waiting for Suzanne to be out of danger and the hunt for the painting to end.

I've chosen not to wait any longer. It won't be easy explaining all this to Sister, especially about the painting in my dream. Maybe, just maybe, she will have a solution.

Margaret had known Sister Agatha for a long time. Through Agatha's friendship and counsel over the years, *Tante* found solutions to many of life's problems. Everyone kept the good nun in prayer after she and Margaret helped to find Patrick's sister, Fiona. Clare called the two of them her angel team.

Rosary beads corded around the waist of a long gray jumper were hidden behind a big white apron, but there was no mistaking Sister Agatha. She still wore the veil of her order. She also wore a smudge of flour across her cheek and along the edge of the starched wimple.

"Ah, *bonjour,* Margaret." Her broad smile was invitation itself. "Come in, *mon ami.*"

"I hope I'm not interrupting your schedule, Sister. I probably should have called ahead, eh?"

"No, no. While the bread is rising, I've been trying to compile notes for a day of reflection. Mother has an assignment for each of us." She rolled her eyes. "We have to multitask these days, you know." Her chuckle belied any real frustration for herself, but a sharp gaze at Margaret and a cocked eyebrow revealed her keen observation. "You look flustered, my dear, or something's different about you, *non?*"

Tante nodded, blushing. "I have a new hairdo, Sister."

"Ah, it's lovely, Margaret. Come into the library and tell me what brings you to us today."

They sat in comfortable reading chairs in front of a small

table piled with books and papers.

Margaret pointed to the items on the table. "Is this your research, Sister?"

"Yes. Each of us is to give a mini talk about the virtues God wants us to aspire to. I chose gentleness. We could choose a saint who inspires that virtue, and I chose Saint Francis de Sales." She tapped on the topmost book on the pile.

Margaret's lips curved into a crooked smile when she looked into the nun's warm brown eyes. "For myself, I would probably have chosen patience."

Words tumbled from Margaret's mouth. She told Sister Agatha about Clare's upcoming wedding, about the Windspirits and the Fontaines, about Jacques's surgery and Kathleen's problem, and lastly, about Paul. When she mentioned the help that Sean Rafferty extended to Paul, Sister's eyes widened.

"You mean *our* Sean Rafferty?"

"*Oui.*" But Margaret continued hurriedly to tell about the dream. She left till last the foremost question on her mind. The dream. "What should I do about the dream?"

Sister Agatha paused, fingers clutching the rosary dangling from beneath her apron. "With all of these problems, Margaret, you prayed for God's will to be done, eh?"

"*Mais oui.* I asked our Lord's help when I talked to Kathleen, and I'm sure He gave me the strength and the right words to convince her."

Sister Agatha nodded, pointing to one of the books on the table. "Saint Francis says, 'Nothing is so strong as gentleness, and nothing so gentle as real strength.' He gave you both when you needed it, my dear."

"That may be, but I didn't have success helping Paul. Paul thought my dream was significant because I've never seen the stolen painting, yet I was able to describe it. He thought my dream was a clue to the location of the painting"—Margaret shook her head—"but the police didn't think my dream was important."

"Ah, Margaret, we don't always get the answers we ask for. Sometimes answers come in surprising ways." Sister Agatha took a scrap of paper from one of the books on the table and folded it into Margaret's hand. "Pray with these words in mind, and I will keep you in my prayers, too. Remember our old pact, my dear? A problem shared is a problem halved."

A clock chimed and Sister Agatha rose. She offered Margaret her arm. "I'm off to the kitchen to check on my bread. Come, *mon ami,* you must take time for tea."

While Sister Agatha shoved six loaves of bread into the large oven, Margaret glanced at the paper in her hand. It was one of Saint Francis's quotations: "My sister, go on steadily and quietly; if the dear Lord means you to run, He will strengthen your heart."

CHAPTER TWENTY-SIX

Paul was in the men's room when Detective Canfield arrived on the third floor. Whether ironically or planned, Canfield and the doctor exited the elevator at the same moment. If there were any new developments, there was no time to share them with Daniel. The detective seemed pretty tight with the doctor, so Daniel said, and they entered Suzanne's room together. The cop on duty said he would let Detective Canfield know that Paul and Daniel would be waiting in the lounge.

Daniel calmly sipped coffee and read the *Tribune,* but Paul was jittery enough without the caffeine. He strode restlessly to the window. The rain made long runnels down the pane, making it difficult to see more than the blinking lights of vehicles in midtown traffic. His mind swarmed with what-ifs.

Did he still trust the Scot? Suzanne put the question in his mind. *Daniel Kelly could have set the whole thing up, but why would he do such a thing? For me to be the fall guy? It doesn't make sense, not with Rafferty pulling the strings. Or does it? What if Rafferty wasn't the true philanthropist he was purported to be?* Paul stared back at Daniel buried in the newspaper. One more day and it would be one week of this nightmare and not a hell of a lot accomplished by Daniel.

Conscious of the nagging ache in his hip and the suspicions he harbored, Paul limped back and sat down. "I haven't said anything to Canfield because Suzanne asked me not to, but something's bugging me about the break-in, and I might as well get it out in the open. Suzanne let the bastard in on the entry phone because she thought the voice sounded like me. She thinks you were behind it, Daniel, setting me up. It took time for me to convince her that wasn't possible."

Daniel jerked to face Paul. His blue eyes darkened with a look that Paul couldn't read. "I don't know whether to laugh or weep for the lady. In all seriousness, Paul, maybe that drug did something to her mind, and more's the pity for it." Daniel closed his eyes, scrubbed his hands over his face, and shook his head in disbelief. "She's a beautiful woman and this morning when I saw her, I actually envied you."

Paul stood, feeling more dejected than ever. "Maybe I'll have a coffee. You want a topper?"

Daniel folded the newspaper and shook his head. "No. I'd like a good look at the crime scene, though. Maroney said the report stated no clear prints on the enterphone. There were no clear prints on the entry phone. My guess is her apartment is no longer sealed."

"Well, Suzanne sure won't be cleaning up the place by herself, and I'm not leaving her this time. It's bad enough that each time I've been with her I got yanked away and shit happened."

Daniel scowled. "Didn't Suzanne tell you? You were in there long enough. I was sure she must have told you the plan."

"Plan? She told me the Feds were arranging a call to the prison, if that's what you're talking about." Paul's eyes narrowed. "But when did *you* get that information?"

"Canfield called my cell while you were in the room with her. Said he was on his way to the hospital. Detective Maroney is out on assignment, and Federal Agent Doyle is undercover on this one. Doyle is going to handle the phone call to Petronelli. That's all I know."

"Doyle? Is he the one that started the investigation when the so-called forgery showed up?"

"Aye, he's the man."

Paul propped his elbows on his thighs and held his head in his hands. "There are too many players. Canfield, Maroney, now Doyle, Richards and whoever went overseas with her." He sat up and shot a questioning look at Daniel. "Richards. What about Richards? They sent her to Interpol, and you said she was a story for another day."

Daniel pursed his lips drawing a long breath. "I prefer to keep the past out of the present."

"Come on. She acts like a sexy bitch. A cold, sexy bitch. Am I right?"

"Aye, but the story ends with you, okay?"

Paul zipped his fingers across his lips.

"When I was investigating Uncle's stolen art incident back in 04, Agent Richards was in the mix of the investigation." Daniel's mouth quirked in a crooked grin. "She came on to me. I know it's hard to believe, me and her, but we did have a whirl in the sheets. I didn't know what she wanted from me other than sex, and I had enough scotch in me not to care. Afterward, I didn't want to find out what she wanted. Word had it that Richards worked her way up to train for the Art Crime Team by diddling the big guys in Washington."

"Bedded her way up? She must have qualified, though—for the Art Crime Team, I mean. She was chosen to go to Italy, for cripes sake!"

"She's highly trained in her field, yes. I'm only talking about her *personal* rise to fame, Paul."

"Well, I wasn't impressed with Richards from the get-go, and Suzanne sure wasn't. Remember how she stood up to her at headquarters the day Canfield ID'd the tail?"

"Aye. Agent Richards met her match intellectually in Miss

Petrone. Let's hope your paramour can hold her own *emotionally* for the duty at hand."

Suzanne was discharged from the hospital at eleven-fifty. The doctor advised a stress-free environment, light diet and rest. She was to call the hospital immediately with any breathing difficulties.

The phone call to her father would have to wait.

Suzanne had remnants of confused thinking, the aftermath of a long unconscious state caused by the overdose. Still she was persistent with two requests. Detective Canfield okayed the first immediately. She would be returned to her apartment, providing she would agree to Agent Doyle's twenty-four-hour surveillance. Wary of the second—which was stronger than a request—Canfield hedged at the outset but, in the end, agreed that Paul Fontaine could be at her side from this point on.

Paul rode with Suzanne in Detective Canfield's vehicle, Daniel following them to the Park Hotel Apartments. "Returning to a crime scene is never easy," Canfield said as he parked in the side parking lot. He glanced in the rearview mirror at the two faces. "I can arrange to have someone come in and clean up the place, Miss Petrone, if you wish. Remember the doctor's orders were no stress."

Suzanne didn't answer. She clung to Paul's arm as they exited the car and followed the detectives into the lobby.

"The entry-phone system has been deactivated temporarily at police request," Canfield continued. "We'll take care of that later, after Agent Doyle is set up in the parking lot."

Suzanne angled her head, studying Paul's face as he stared at the phone. An involuntary shake of his head, and her fingers clutched his arm tighter. He felt her shudder when they exited the elevator and Detective Canfield threw open the apartment door.

Paul guided Suzanne straight through the foyer to the circular leather sofa in the living room. He bent over to right an upended table and watched fear cloud her eyes. He followed the direction of her eyes back to the foyer. Detective Canfield stood in the entry talking to Daniel.

"Daniel is my transportation, and he's not to be worried about," Paul said, raising his shoulders in a questioning shrug. "Sit tight here for a minute while I go see what's up."

The three men moved out into the corridor, leaving the door slightly ajar. Suzanne could hear muffled voices. The detective's husky drawl, the PI's soft Scottish burr, and Paul's distinct voice.

"What about the other apartment on this floor?" Daniel asked.

Canfield pointed with his thumb. "The occupants of 201 were duly advised about the situation. They're an elderly retired couple, left on an Elderhostel flight to Mexico this morning. There will be no trouble on second floor. The office and the manager's suite occupy the first floor. Everything's been taken care of."

"What about Agent Doyle? I saw a van pull in as I entered the building. Looked like him."

"That's him, setting up. I'll check in with him on my way out." Detective Canfield turned his gaze to Paul. "Daniel's willing to come back here mid-morning tomorrow." Dan nodded, giving Paul a thumbs-up. "You up for this, Fontaine?" Canfield asked.

"Damned straight I am." Paul nodded. "Wouldn't have it otherwise." Paul started to push open the door, but Canfield's hand stopped him.

"I'm going to precede you into Miss Petrone's, into the bedroom for one last look around before it gets put in order. The crime-scene boys are good, but I get the last look."

The detective put a hand on Daniel's shoulder. "Our officers took a class from a very sharp lady lawyer. It was called the 'Art of Perception.' " Canfield shot him an easy smile. "Helps ya fine-tune details. I'm going to test what I learned. Might be helpful to y'all in the future, Daniel. Remind me to give you her business card."

Canfield cocked an eyebrow at Paul and spoke in a voice just above a whisper. "I expect you will stay out of the bedroom after you've tidied it up, Fontaine. I'm sure y'all know what I mean," he said. "Doctor's orders, okay?"

Paul held his tongue, nodded and followed the men into the apartment.

Suzanne's head was tipped back and the sleek fall of ruler-straight hair fanned out, shining jet-black against the sofa. Her eyes were closed. As soon as Canfield and Daniel were out of sight, Paul sat beside her, lifted his hand to touch her cheek. Her eyes opened lazily. "God, but you're beautiful," he whispered.

Her hazel eyes had lost their spark. "I don't feel beautiful. I feel wasted, confused and afraid." She reached for his hand. "The only thing I'm sure of is you. I want you beside me."

He lifted her hand to his lips, kissed her fingers one by one. "I will be. Count on it."

Paul stood. Placing his hands under her arms he lifted and pulled Suzanne, propping her against a pillow at one end of the sofa. He removed her shoes and squeezed her toes. "Put your feet up, my lady, and rest here on the sofa until the big guys leave." He motioned to the bedroom with his head. "Canfield is taking a last look around in there, and Daniel will probably leave with him. Meantime, I'll get to work in the kitchen. I'll try to put things right until you're feeling well enough to give me direction, okay?"

CHAPTER TWENTY-SEVEN

The ring tone sounded like the funky clock radio Molly had given him during the storm. Paul reached and patted a tabletop, trying to find the clock and turn it off. *Glass table? What the hell?* His eyes opened to stare at a painting on the wall beyond a long, oval glass-topped table beside him. Paul sat up on the leather sofa, trying to bring his surroundings into focus. A cell phone was ringing somewhere on the far side of the table stretched front and center of the U-shaped sectional sofa he was lying on. "Crap," he mumbled, and dashed around the table, stumbling over his shoes, to search for the phone. He found the phone in a jumble of clothes at the other end of the sofa.

"Morning, Paul. Daniel here."

"Oh, God. Afraid I'm a little disoriented, Dan. I thought I was waking up on Casey Key."

"I left there twenty minutes ago. The Key is looking pretty good after the storm. I called to give you a heads-up that I'll be there in about ten minutes. Molly packed your duffel with clean clothes. I'll be stoppin' at Agent Doyle's van, then I'm comin' up to the apartment. Be ready." The phone disconnected.

Paul checked his watch. Nine-forty-five. He pulled jeans out of the clothes pile and headed for the small bathroom near the kitchen. Minutes later he emerged to hear a shower running beyond Suzanne's door. He finger combed his hair and dashed back to the sofa to pull on his shirt. The quilt he slept with lay

188

balled up on the floor. A knock at the door had him folding it quickly.

Daniel entered the living room, followed by a man. "Agent Doyle, meet Paul Fontaine."

Doyle didn't look like the suit-and-tie FBI guys you see on TV, but then, Paul remembered, he was undercover. He shook his hand. "I'm guessing your night out there was uneventful, Agent Doyle, and you're here to speak with Suzanne?"

"Not uneventful, no." The agent scanned the room. "I'm here because both of you need to hear what I have to say. Detective Canfield wanted to give Miss Petrone more time, but that's not possible now."

Daniel caught Paul's frown. He cleared his throat and handed Paul the duffel. "Molly sends her regards and says to tell you the Jacuzzi is back on."

Paul couldn't help but smile. "I hope there's a toothbrush in here," he said.

"Aye, Molly's thorough." Daniel eyed the quilt on the sofa. "Did you have a comfortable night, Paul?"

Paul grinned. "I did."

Paul heard the footsteps first, quickly lost his grin, and all heads turned to Suzanne. She paused beside a small bistro table and chairs in an alcove at the end of the room. Outside the alcove window sunlight broke through dark clouds, spinning light into the room. Suzanne stood at the window watching sunlight shimmer on rain-glistened leaves of a huge live-oak tree at window height. She turned from the view, one hand holding tightly to a chair. Her gaze shot from Paul to the two men standing in her living room. She sat down and continued to stare stonily at them.

Paul moved quickly to her side. "Guess I forgot to mention that Daniel would be coming by this morning." He held up the duffel still in his hand. "He brought my things from the Key and, uh . . ."

"I know Agent Doyle," she interrupted. "Sorry not to welcome you, but it's a little unsettling to have guests before breakfast, especially if you aren't a morning person, and I'm not. If you've come about the phone call—"

"I'm not here about the phone call, Miss Petrone." Doyle's gaze shot from Suzanne to Paul. "I've had communication from the American consulate in Milan. CID agrees that you should be advised regarding developments there, but rather than wait for Detective Canfield, I decided to come up with Detective Kelly to explain."

Paul nodded, but Suzanne sat tight-lipped and motionless.

"To recap a little for your understanding, Interpol had issued a previous red notice on the alleged American courier who smuggled the Monet painting into Italy. The Carabinieri are the most successful art squad worldwide, and they figured heavily in his arrest."

Paul's mind was spinning. *Son of a bitch—given a chance, so could Tante's dream put them there.*

"Whoa," Paul said, looking at Daniel. "Red notice?"

Daniel jumped in. "That's the foreign version of an all-points bulletin."

Agent Doyle cleared his throat. "You know, of course, that Agents Richards and Flynn were supported over there by our special trial attorneys?" Paul did a mental eye roll, nodded to Doyle and stole a glance at Suzanne. *No wonder she's so testy with FBI. She's probably relating all this stuff to her father's arrest.*

"Our legal team moved quickly for the extradition of the American suspect, and in short order it was granted."

Paul blew out an audible "Phew and Halleluiah."

Doyle's eyes tracked to Suzanne. She opened her mouth and closed it. He continued without pause. "At seventeen-hundred yesterday, Agents Richards and Flynn transported the suspect to Melpensa airport for a night flight to DC. Thirty minutes before their flight boarded, the suspect was shot and killed in the terminal."

It's worse than a nightmare. It's diabolic and vicious. My father behind bars, Paul attacked, I'm attacked, now a murder. It has to end. The voices in Suzanne's head were drowning out the voices of the others in the room.

Detective Canfield arrived minutes after Doyle's bombshell message. It was obvious he was pissed that Doyle didn't wait for him. After a few choice words Doyle left for his van immediately. Daniel followed suit, claiming he had business to take care of.

Suzanne didn't move from her chair. She stared at dust motes dancing in spilled sunshine on the glass tabletop. She listened to Detective Canfield's gravelly drawl. "Suppose ya'll could make coffee, Fontaine? I surely would welcome a cup." Suzanne's lips curved in a weak smile.

Paul set mugs and spoons on the table and started the coffeemaker. Canfield walked to the open bedroom door, paused to look in, and returned to Suzanne's side. "Mind if I sit, Miss Petrone? We still need to make sense of this break-in. I know the timing's bad, but Agent Doyle . . ." He shrugged, shook his head and eased his long-legged, lanky frame onto the small chair. "I was hoping we could backtrack a little, step by step, to give you a frame of reference for your talk with your father."

He caught a disapproving frown from Paul, but continued. "I'd like to hear your thoughts about what happened here two days ago. We haven't had an opportunity to talk about it."

Suzanne watched Paul drag a stool from the kitchen. He perched on it, pursed his lips and closed his eyes in a barely perceptible nod to her.

She took a slow, hitching breath. "Okay. You looked in my

bedroom, Detective, so you know Paul cleaned up the mess last night. He put back the Cezanne that was torn from the wall." She shot a weak smile at him. "Hangs a little crooked, but then, I think Paul's theory was right. Whoever pulled it off my bedroom wall was probably looking for a wall safe. A serious art thief would know that the Cezanne was just a nicely framed copy. I think someone was looking for something in here, but nothing was taken."

Suzanne clutched her hands together, stared out the window for a few seconds before she returned her gaze to Canfield. "I don't understand the drug. Why would someone want to drug me?"

"Why indeed," Canfield said, nodding. "We're talking now about what happened *after* you were drugged. What about before? Do you remember being called on the entry phone?"

Suzanne shot an uneasy glance at Paul. She couldn't lie. "I thought it was Paul, but the voice was muffled. I'd been waiting for him, and I just buzzed him in without thinking."

"Anyone else know Mr. Fontaine was going to visit you?"

Paul couldn't sit still any longer. He jumped up. "Only Daniel knew it. You know it wasn't me, Detective, and it sure as hell wasn't Daniel. I made the call to the precinct from Kelly's car because Suzanne didn't answer her phone. It's on record, for Christ's sake." Paul huffed out a breath, stomped into the kitchen and brought coffee to the table.

"Anything else, Mr. Fontaine? On or off the record?"

"Yes, as a matter of fact, since you're backtracking. My aunt's dream identified the real painting and placed it in a foreign country before the authentic Monet was recovered in Italy. Remember that? Remember my theory, Detective? I told you about the dream and the forgery. Monet's *Argenteuil* that showed up in Sarasota was a forgery, meant to muddy the trail while the real thing was on its way overseas."

"I remember your theory, and it's a pretty good one. We know the syndicate is still at work in Florida, but the alleged forgery hasn't surfaced, nor the perp. There's a missing link, ya see. A fox in the henhouse, Mr. Fontaine"—Canfield's eyes shifted from Paul to Suzanne—"but we're bound to flush him out."

Minutes passed as Canfield sipped his coffee thoughtfully. "I think we've tired Miss Petrone enough for today. I'd like to leave you with something to think about this morning. It's a verse from the Bible, a favorite one of my momma's. She often quoted it to me when I first joined the force." He pointed to his head. "It stuck and it kinda fits here." His face broke into a slow smile. "That is, if you have no objection to a cop quoting scripture." Detective Canfield raised an eyebrow, angling his head toward Paul.

Surprised, Paul shook his head. "None from me."

"It's from Matthew, scolding the Pharisees: 'You strain your water so you would not swallow a gnat, then you swallow a camel.' "

The detective chuckled at Paul's puzzled face. "Took me a while, too," he said, easing his long legs up from the small bistro chair. He tapped twice on the glass tabletop. "Easy does it Miss Petrone. Talk to y'all later."

Paul's cell phone rang as soon as the door closed on Detective Canfield. He was both relieved and anxious when he saw the readout. It was his father. "Hi, Pa. Been waiting for your call. Everything okay?"

"I meant to call you as soon as I came home from the hospital, and I'm sorry, Paul, but any excuse would sound lame, now. Things just don't always go as smoothly as planned."

"That's for sure. Does Doc think you're making a good recovery?"

"Yes, I'm healing well and my appetite's back. I had a surprise, though, yesterday, and you were part of it, Paul."

"A surprise?"

"I had a phone call from Sean Rafferty. Somehow I think Margaret had something to do with it. Nevertheless it was a pleasant, reassuring call. He said he realized you were my son, and wanted to assure me that you were in good hands in Florida. He told me the stolen painting was found. I'm relieved for you, son. Rafferty said authorities would be wrapping things up now. I was real grateful he thought to call me, and I hope that means you'll be home soon."

Beyond surprise, Paul stammered. "Well . . . uh . . . soon, Pa. Yeah, soon. I'm trying to straighten out a few things here and—"

"If it's your friend you're worrying about, Margaret told me about Suzanne. She said you two have a lot in common. We'd like to meet her, son. Also, Margaret says Clare is counting on you for the wedding, so let us know if we can help with flight arrangements."

Paul sat staring at the cell phone. For a minute he wasn't capable of thought.

CHAPTER TWENTY-EIGHT

Daniel's drive back down SR 41 wasn't exactly peaceful. No yammering from Fontaine to divert his thoughts, but all the action from the last twenty-four hours replayed in his head.

Yesterday's phone call from Boston had to be the biggest break so far. Uncle's fax to Milan must have speeded up the extradition proceedings, no doubt about that. But Uncle couldn't possibly know about the airport yet. Too soon for him to have heard about the shooting. Doyle only got the wire this morning, and he was waiting on Richards or Flynn and the Carabinieri. More important was the painting. Would it come back with them?

Tomorrow, Doyle said. No later than tomorrow the call would go to Otisville prison in New York. Meantime, Canfield was in his office waiting on lab results—something found in Suzanne's bedroom that Daniel wasn't privy to. Sit tight, he said. A couple jiggers of scotch might make the sittin' easier.

Maybe I'll drive by Rob's studio and see what the phone call Molly took is all about. Daniel clicked on his iPod. Time for a little Mozart.

Detective Canfield held the bag up to the light, focusing on the barely visible content. A single hair. He pictured Suzanne's long, shiny black hair. CS techs found strands of Ms. Petrone's hair on the bed, but not this one. *Have to give that Amy gal credit.* "I'll teach you to fine-tune details," she said. *Yep, even an old buck like me learned somethin' from that perception class. I wouldn't have found this snagged in the frame if I wasn't studying the painting in Miss Petrone's bedroom.*

He tossed the evidence bag on his desk and looked up from under bushy eyebrows at Detective Maroney walking into his office.

" 'Bout time." Canfield said.

" 'Bout time, shit! Give me a break. I flew to New Orleans, and I'm back in two days. It's like being in a different country over there. The chief wasn't what you'd call cooperative either. Not until I pulled out the FBI file."

"Yeah, yeah. Know all about NOPD. So? You had a kick-ass grin when you came in here." Canfield tapped on the evidence bag. "Did he sing?"

Maroney twisted his lips into a wide smile and wiggled his eyebrows. "Got the man and got a name! He caved when I named our source and told him the charges he's facing. He's downstairs in lockup, waitin' on his lawyer."

Canfield couldn't help but grin. "Hot damn, Maroney! I thought maybe you had it in ya, an' ya came up aces." Detective Canfield tucked the evidence bag inside his suit coat. "Now, before anything leaks over to agent Doyle, let's go downstairs and see what we can do."

Brant's studio was locked up tight, a CLOSED sign painted on plywood covering the glass at the front of the building. The high window on the Gulf side was boarded up, too. *Never knew him to be so cautious,* Daniel said to himself.

Reggae music could be heard from the Cove a short block away. He had no problem finding a parking spot at midday. *Most regulars are probably still cleaning up their boats or beachfront.* Daniel couldn't miss Rob sitting alone in the tiki bar. He pulled up a stool next to him and nodded to the bartender. "I'll have the usual, Jake. Buy you a drink, Rob?" he asked, pointing to Rob's glass.

The bartender caught Daniel's eye with a little shake of his head as he poured two fingers of scotch over ice.

Rob Brant's eyes narrowed when he turned to Daniel. "Where the hell you been?" he asked.

Daniel returned his stare, puzzled by his tone of voice. "Molly said you called this morning, but I haven't had time to get back to you till now. I stopped by your studio, saw the boarded up windows."

Brant slugged the last of his vodka. "Yeah, well, got to protect, you know. Isn't that what you do, Detective?" He swiveled on the stool, threw an arm out toward the Gulf. "Protect your uncle's property?"

Something's wrong, Daniel thought. *The guy's hair is wild, not tied back neat like usual. He's got a two-day growth of beard and he's snockered.*

"Aye, Molly and I take care of Seaview. Is that what you called about this morning?"

Brant snorted, shook his head. "Called about your client. The gallery director you're babysitting."

Daniel sipped his scotch. "I don't take kindly to the inference, Rob, but I'll chalk it up. What is it you're wanting to know about Fontaine?"

"Where is he? Molly says he's not at Seaview anymore."

"Molly is loose-lipped sometimes, and she's not always accurate. I'm on my way to the house now. I just stopped in for a quick one." Daniel finished his drink and stood. "Can I give you a lift somewhere?"

Rob shook his head. "Nope. Stayin' right here till it's over."

Daniel moved to the end of the bar, more puzzled than ever. "What's wrong with him, Jake? I've not seen him like this before. He must know Hurricane Sybil moved out two days ago."

"Yeah, he does. He's been in and out of here steady since the storm tracked northwest. He knows it's over." Jake shrugged. "I don't think that's what he means. He seems depressed or something. Keeps talking about closing shop, and getting off the Key. Today he's been at the booze pretty heavy, and he seems different than usual. Don't know what else to tell you, man."

They ordered Chinese takeout. Paul laughed when Suzanne tried to teach him to eat moo goo gai pan with chopsticks. "Guess I'll either starve or eat caveman style," he said. "Give me a lobster anytime, and I'd have no problem crackin' at it, but these . . ." He twirled the sticks between his fingers then tossed them aside. "Are useless." Paul finished his food with a fork.

"First thing we're going to do when I take you to Maine is go to DiMillo's in Old Port and have a lobster dinner. We'll wash it down with champagne, then we'll go to Francois's Fancy to meet the family." Paul smiled, raising his eyebrows inquisitively. "Sound like a plan?"

Suzanne nodded. "You sound so positive. How do you know your family will even want to meet me?"

Paul talked as he cleared the table. "Because my father has already asked to meet you, and my sister Maddy, too. She's my only sibling, and we're close. Her husband Patrick is a great guy. Then there's *Tante* Margaret. She and Clare are like extended family. My father trusts Margaret with his life, and so do I. She is the only person who knew about you before I left. *Tante* Margaret is my promise keeper."

"Is she your father's sister?"

"No." Paul grinned, taking Suzanne's hands to pull her away from the table. "She's Clare's aunt, but we all call her *Tante*. Actually, she's Clare's surrogate mom, and Clare is Maddy's best friend. It's complicated, my sweet, but trust me, you're going to love them."

Paul cradled her in his arms. "We're talking about afterward . . . after this mess is over and we're out of here." He cupped her face in his hands. "But this is now, and I want very much to love you, Suzanne." His kiss was slow, soft and sweet. "Are you okay with that? Can I try to make the fears go away?" He traced fingertips slowly down her arms.

Smiling, Suzanne reached her arms around his neck. "I thought you'd never ask."

CHAPTER TWENTY-NINE

Stretched out beside her, Paul propped himself on one elbow to gaze at Suzanne. *God, but she's beautiful.* He thought of kissing her awake, but this was the morning she was dreading. He rose carefully and left the bedroom as quietly as possible.

The kitchen stove clock read seven-thirty. He pulled a neatly folded silk shirt from his duffel bag and draped it over the kitchen bar stool. *Nice choice, Molly.* He pulled out his toiletry kit and headed for the powder room. *Daniel doesn't know how lucky he is having Molly at Seaview.*

Ten minutes later Paul was lathered up to shave when the house phone rang. He made it to the kitchen on the third ring and carefully lifted the receiver. Suzanne's sleepy voice was mumbling hello.

"Agent Doyle, here. Sorry to be early, Miss Petrone, but there is a change of plans you should know about. Pending Agent Richard's flight arrival in Tampa, Detective Canfield will be arranging a conference at headquarters later."

"Is this for the call to my father?" she asked.

Paul waited, not daring to breathe, through a pause that followed. "No. There are new developments, and the phone call will not be necessary." Paul could hear anger in Doyle's clipped words. "SPD will be monitoring your entry phone from my position here, so you should be secure until an escort is arranged for you. Your next call will be from Detective Canfield."

Paul waited for the click before he hung up the receiver and bounded into the bedroom. He sat beside her on the bed, pulled her close and pressed his cheek to hers. "Doyle sounded like one mad SOB, but who cares. The phone call is off. Are you relieved?"

Puzzled, Suzanne frowned, pointed a finger at him. "Yes, but how did you know?"

He pushed her shoulders back gently against the headboard and kissed her forehead, then covered her lips in a noisy kiss. "I listened on the kitchen phone. New developments, he said! That's gotta be good, huh? Canfield must have something going at the division to change the phone-call plan."

Suzanne sank down into the pillows, laughing and nodding her head. "Oh, Paul. Shaving cream is smeared all over your face." She swiped two fingers down her cheek, holding them up. "And now I'm wearing half of it." She pasted the slippery lather on Paul's nose, kissed his lips carefully, laughing harder than ever. "You better go shave."

Paul wrapped her in his arms, chuckling. "Forget the shave. Eavesdropping brought better results."

Daniel was eating a late lunch at the kitchen counter. As soon as he came in from the Cove, he told Molly in no uncertain terms she should reveal nothing on the phone about Paul's whereabouts to anyone except his uncle Sean.

"But Mister is a friend," she argued.

"Friend or foe, you give no information on the phone. You simply ask if you can take a message."

The kitchen phone rang as if on cue, and Molly rolled her eyes. "Are you at home, Sir Daniel?" she asked, doing a little curtsey. Daniel nodded, and Molly picked up the receiver. "Seaview." Seconds later she said, "One minute, please," covering the receiver with her hand. "Says his name is Jake, and he wants to speak with you."

Daniel stood, his hand outstretched for the phone. He carried it out to the lanai. "What's up, Jake?"

"Your friend. I think he might be in trouble. He left right after you did and came back cleaned up a little. He asked me to keep something for him till tomorrow. I don't generally hold things, ya know, but you saw how he was earlier. He's been getting pretty ugly on the booze, and I didn't want trouble. Brant took a leather case from his jacket and laid it on the bar. Said it was too important to carry around, so I agreed to stash it in my lockbox for overnight."

"Did he say where he was going?"

"Nope. Just said he had to see a man about a painting. I had bad vibes about the leather case. It felt kind of heavy, ya know, so when he left, I checked inside it. Plane tickets in there didn't surprise me 'cause Rob's been talking about leavin' the Key, but the thirty-eight Smith and Wesson was a jolt. I got to thinkin' about that piece, and it bugged me. I thought maybe somebody should know, an' yer the first person came to mind."

"I'm glad you called, Jake. This is as big a surprise to me as it is to you. I'll have to dig around, see what I can find. Meantime, we'll keep it between us, okay?"

Daniel returned the phone to the kitchen. "I'll not be finishing my lunch, Molly. I'll be in my room on the computer if anyone should call, and I'll be traveling up to Sarasota again in a little while. That's not to be told either, unless it's Uncle calling."

It didn't take long to browse the Net and find the dealer's gallery where the forged painting was purportedly taken for sale. He remembered it was a big one off Main Street, but it helped to know the gallery owner's name. He jotted it in his notebook beside the dealer's name Brant gave him. His watch said three-fifteen.

Thirty minutes later, Daniel pulled into a parking space a

block away from Main Street. Luckily it was "Friday Night Stroll," and all the merchants were open for business until eight P.M.

He approached a well-dressed, older gentleman standing in the rear of the large gallery. "Mr. Fitzsimmons? My name is Daniel Kelly." He flashed his ID. "I'd like to speak to Joseph Scavone."

The man shook his head, smiling. "I'm not Mr. Fitzsimmons. I'm his father-in-law. Just filling in this week while Donald's on a buying trip. As to Joseph Scavone, he's no longer with us."

"Can you tell me where I might locate Mr. Scavone?"

The man nodded. "I'm told he took an appraiser's job at a fine-arts auction house in New Orleans. Seems more people are selling collections these days, with the economy so bad."

"Would you have an address for him?"

The old guy cocked his head as though he were thinking. "There was a young man like yourself in here a few days ago asking the same question. Sorry, but I don't have that information."

Daniel walked a block back to his car. *Young man? That leaves Canfield out. Could have been Maroney or Doyle.* He pulled out his cell phone and dialed crime division headquarters. The desk told him that Detective Canfield was occupied in conference. Daniel headed straight for Ringling Boulevard.

He sat in the cramped waiting area. Luckily the corporal on duty recognized him, didn't bug him about waiting, and even sent a message to Canfield's desk that Kelly was there. After what seemed a long wait to Dan, the corporal signaled him to go on up.

Agent Doyle gave him a cursory nod when Daniel came through the door. "Glad you showed up, Kelly," Detective Canfield said. "I tried to track you down earlier, but your housekeeper at Seaview wouldn't tell me squat."

Kelly frowned. "When was this?"

"Less than an hour ago," the detective said, eyeing Doyle. "We need some info from you before we go into conference with the DA."

Daniel looked from Canfield to Doyle. "The DA? Not sure I follow."

"Plea bargaining, Daniel. We need the DA for plea bargaining. Miss Petrone's daddy came through for us, just as we suspected he might." Canfield shot a glance at Doyle. "We tracked the initial contact in the case and Maroney made an arrest."

Daniel looked at Doyle. A muscle in the agent's jaw twitched, but Doyle neither met Daniel's gaze nor responded to Canfield. His eyes were on notes in a folder on his lap.

"Are you talking about the art dealer who called in the forgery?"

Canfield smiled and nodded. "You got it. With confirmation from Anthony Petronelli"—Canfield cleared his throat, shooting a glance at Doyle—"and with agent Doyle's profile on him, Maroney brought the suspect in. Agent Doyle is looking at statutes under Title Eighteen, but presently, we have Joseph Scavone booked on aiding and abetting a federal crime and . . . fraud."

"Fraud? You talking about the forgery?"

"Mm-hm," Detective Canfield scratched his head. "In a manner of speaking, yes. Your client, Fontaine, was pretty much on track when he claimed the forgery was a diversion scheme. He was right about that. Thing is, where was the forgery?"

Daniel fingered his mustache, hardly able to credit his ears. He looked at Doyle, then back at Canfield.

"We didn't find the fraudulent Monet," Canfield said. "But Joseph Scavone knew where it came from. He reported it, then spirited it away. It was a syndicate scheme to keep the trail here in Florida while the authentic painting was transported to Italy.

That's why your information is needed right now, Kelly."

Daniel shook his head. "I don't have anything on Scavone."

"Scavone gave us the collaborator who painted the fraudulent Monet. That's what criminals do when they're caught, eh. They sing. Checks out that Agent Doyle has a profile on the accomplice." Canfield kept his gaze on Daniel. "He's an artist, lives on Casey Key, name of Robert Brant."

The bartender's phone call and his encounter with Brant earlier flashed through Daniel's mind, but still, he couldn't believe it. He shook his head, facing Agent Doyle. "Doesn't make sense. I know Brant pretty well. Why would FBI have a profile on him?"

"He was questioned in a two-thousand-four stabbing death of a gallery owner in Sarasota. He was a person of interest in the case, so his prints are on file," Doyle said.

"Does Brant know your client, Paul Fontaine?" Canfield asked.

Daniel's usual *in-control* voice faded to a soft Scottish slur. "Aye, but what's that to do with—"

"Did he know about Fontaine's relationship to Miss Petrone?"

Daniel nodded.

"I have evidence that connects Brant to the break-in at Miss Petrone's apartment."

Daniel's body stiffened. His eyes narrowed in a scowl as he considered Canfield's words.

"Brant had to have motive," Canfield continued. "Why do you think he did it? Keep an open mind, Daniel. Without an open mind, you run the risk of excluding the real deal. Sit down and tell us what you know about Brant and Miss Petrone."

Daniel chose his words carefully. "Most of what I know is what Brant told me. I met him in a local bar shortly after he opened his studio on the south end of the Key. Said he came down here to get away from Sarasota and the crime scene on

Palm Avenue. We knew about the gallery stabbing that happened right after we came to Casey Key, so his reasoning sounded logical.

"Brant sold some paintings to Mrs. Rafferty, and we became a little better acquainted. When my uncle's paintings were stolen, he gave me some tips about the art black market. That helped me to proceed with my investigation. You guys must remember my uncle's robbery case. That's how I met you, Detective Canfield."

Canfield nodded. "I remember, but let's cut to the chase, Daniel. What about Brant's relationship with Miss Petrone?"

"My knowledge, again, is secondhand. Brant saw her at Ringling right after she was interrogated about the painting. She thought she was being followed. He said she was scared and needed someone she could trust. He called me, and I found out that she *was* being followed. Maybe Rob pursued the relationship after that." Daniel shrugged. "Your guess is as good as mine. She is a beautiful woman."

"That's all you know about the relationship?"

Daniel hesitated. "They knew each other from the year before. Brant taught a class for local young artists, and Suzanne posed for the class. Nude. The painting of Miss Petrone wound up in a co-op gallery in Sarasota, and I brought Paul Fontaine to see it right after he arrived at Seaview."

"And why was that, Daniel?" Canfield asked.

"Because Fontaine came here to find Miss Petrone. My uncle brought him down here, as you probably know, because her painting was stolen from Cornerstone Gallery. I initiated Paul's pursuit of Miss Petrone by showing him Brant's painting, as a possible lead to find her. After he saw it, he was pretty insistent about meeting Brant."

"How'd that go?"

Daniel shook his head. "I wasn't privy to the meeting, but

Paul was pretty upset when it was over. I don't know what else I can tell you. You gotta know by now that Miss Petrone is pretty serious about Fontaine, and likewise."

Agent Doyle hadn't said a word. After Daniel's last words, he nodded to Canfield and picked up his notebook and folders. "I think we have what we need," he said. "I'll be at the field office."

As soon as he left the room, Detective Canfield rose and clamped a hand on Daniel's shoulder. "Thank you, Daniel. Stay alert, my friend, and stay in touch. We may need you again real soon."

CHAPTER THIRTY

Suzanne fastened a silver barrette in her hair and turned to face Paul. "I guess I'm ready," she said, stepping away from the dresser.

Paul grasped her hand and spoke softly. "Just remember that whatever Canfield says about your father, it won't alter our plans. I know you're hoping for the best for him, but if the painting is secure, we're on the first plane out of here." He tilted her chin up to look into her eyes. "Okay?"

Suzanne nodded, and they walked together into the living room. Paul had let Detective Canfield in minutes before, while Suzanne was changing her clothes. The detective rose from the sofa when she approached.

"Miss Petrone." He nodded.

"Sorry to keep you waiting, Detective. Please sit down." Suzanne looked at the empty sofa. "Only the three of us, Detective? What happened to the conference?"

"Agent Richards deplaned with a flu-like illness this afternoon, and I'll get to her in a minute, but I 'spect y'all won't mind if Agent Doyle isn't here with me." Canfield grinned. "He's up at the field office, and he wouldn't need to hear about the prison phone call one more time, anyway."

"Wasn't it his plan for me to speak with my father in a conference call?" Suzanne asked.

"That was Agent Doyle's plan, yes, but I preempted it, you see. I was following a hunch about a suspect that the FBI had no profile on, and it paid off. I called the prison warden myself, Miss Petrone, without waiting for Agent Doyle." Canfield paused, watching her carefully. "I spoke very frankly with your father about your condition and the danger you are in."

Suzanne's eyes filled with tears. "Was he . . . did he—"

"Your father is very concerned about you. He willingly confirmed that the suspect I named was a contact of his here in Florida." Canfield smiled, nodding. "That contact proved my hunch to be correct, ya see. It helped to break the case, so we will be meeting with your father's attorney next week to talk about a possible appeal."

"Oh, God." Suzanne gulped back a sob, wiped tears away with her fingers. "Sorry, but I was really dreading that call, and this is such a relief."

"The contact," Paul asked, "was it someone local? Does his arrest tie in to the break-in?"

Canfield shot Paul a look. "The break-in is still being investigated. You were almost right, Mr. Fontaine, with your theory. The forgery was a diversional tactic."

Paul grabbed Suzanne's hand. Their eyes met as they shared an incredible moment of silent understanding, but Detective Canfield was quick to break the silence. "Your father allegedly knew nothing about the forgery plan, Miss Petrone. That may be in his favor when the authentic painting is returned."

"*When* it's returned? Didn't Agent Richards bring it back?" Suzanne asked.

"She did, but as I said, Miss Richards is in sick bay. Agent Doyle secured the painting for her at the Tampa Field Office. I think it has to have some final assessment before it is removed from the Stolen Art File in New York City and returned to your gallery, Fontaine. Agent Doyle was a little vague with me about that."

Paul checked his watch. "Does Daniel know about any of

this, Detective?"

Detective Canfield's voice sounded raspier than usual. His head waggled back and forth. "Some of it, yes."

Paul put an arm around Suzanne's shoulders. "We should go down to the Key, talk to Daniel and maybe phone Mr. Rafferty."

Detective Canfield stood and cleared his throat. "You might not find Detective Kelly available. There are extenuating circumstances that I presume Daniel is working on."

It was late, but Daniel set his mind to the task. He mentally rehashed anything and everything about Rob Brant that could connect the artist to the break-in or the so-called forgery. He started with Agent Doyle's profile.

Brant admitted to being befriended by a gallery owner who was stabbed to death, so that made him a person of interest in that crime before I knew him. I thought naught of it at the time.

Brant admittedly had questionable friends on the wrong end of art deals. How else could he put the finger on Uncle's stolen painting showing up for barter on the black market? I didn't question his sources then, either.

Brant vouched for the art dealer who claimed the Monet brought to him was a forgery. He steered me away from him, and I didn't pursue the dealer.

Three times he called the house since Paul arrived. Brant's relationship with Suzanne could have been more than it seemed. She was at his studio posing last year and was back again when she needed help this year. I never made the connection. Why didn't I see this coming?

Daniel checked with Jake at the tiki bar as soon as he got home. He left his car ouside in case he had to make a fast trip, but Jake said Brant hadn't returned for the leather case. Where would he go? If he did try to contact Scavone, then he might have been tipped off about his arrest.

For the first time, Daniel felt regret. Guile was not in his character, nor deceit, but the job called for it. He knew Brant had a sister nearby and they were close. She was a young single mom, with a kid and no husband. He searched white pages on the Net until it spewed out her address and phone number in Bradenton. He punched in the number on his cell phone.

"Miss, I'm calling about your brother's studio on Casey Key. I haven't been able to reach him since the hurricane. The business is closed, and no one's seen him."

Her voice sounded young and timid. "Are you a friend of Rob's?"

"Yes, ma'am. Well, a patron at least. My family bought some of his earlier work and . . . well, Rob showed me a painting of you and him when you were young. That's how I thought of calling you. I'd like to commission a painting like that for my family, but his shop being boarded up had me concerned. I wondered if something happened to him."

"Oh, no. You needn't worry about that. Rob is okay, and I'm sure he'll be painting again soon. When I see him, shall I tell him who called?"

"Thank you kindly, ma'am, but as long as I know your brother is still in business, I'll try him later."

After ending the call, Daniel considered it for less than a minute. He dialed Canfield's cell phone.

Riding in the back of an unmarked police car for the second time in a week was not something either Paul or Suzanne wanted to do. Detective Canfield insisted that Suzanne might still be in danger. The intruder had not been found, so when Paul insisted on returning to Casey Key, Detective Canfield said it was a protective measure for him to take them there.

With Detective Maroney driving, it took less time than usual to get out of the city and down SR 41. The only reminder Paul thought to give him was to watch for the sign that said Casey Key—Nokomis Beach, then turn right. Otherwise, with Maroney's heavy foot, they could have zipped right by the road.

Paul was surprised to see Daniel's Ford parked in the driveway when the detective pulled into Seaview. "I thought you told us Daniel probably wouldn't be available?" he said to Detective Canfield.

"Well, you're in luck then, aren't you," Canfield said. "Looks like maybe Kelly came home in a hurry. Detective Maroney and I have some business down this way, and I do believe y'all are safe here at Mr. Rafferty's. We'll wait to see that you get inside and check back with you in a while."

Paul led Suzanne to the garage side door and rang the bell. They waited in Canfield's headlights until Molly opened the door. Paul waved and Maroney backed out of the driveway.

Molly's face was full of surprise. "Oh, my! Good evenin' to ya, Paul, and to the lovely lady. I don't think Daniel is expecting you, but come right along now." She led the way to the elevator.

"I wasn't expecting Daniel to be here," Paul said, "until I saw his car outside. Molly, this is Suzanne. We won't be in your way long. I need to pack up my things and talk with Daniel and Mr. Rafferty."

They were entering the kitchen as Paul spoke, and Molly stood still as a stone, looking from Suzanne to Paul. "I hope yer not meanin' to leave us for good. Daniel has been locked up in his room with orders not to disturb him, and Mr. Rafferty hasn't given me any notice about yer leavin' Seaview."

"Not to worry, Molly. I'll be calling Mr. Rafferty myself, and as for Daniel, well, I'll take my chances and knock on his door."

"That won't be necessary," Daniel said, walking into the living room. "I heard the bell and the elevator. How did you get here, Paul?"

"Canfield brought us. Said he didn't think you'd be available. I came to pack my things. I was intending to let your uncle know that I'll be in Sarasota until we can get flight arrangements." Paul took Suzanne's hand and moved close to Daniel's side. "We haven't told Canfield about the flight plans. He still thinks Suzanne is in danger, but I don't see it that way."

Daniel swiped a hand over his face. "Molly, we won't be needing you now. We'll be on the lanai, and should anyone ring, I'll answer. Come." He motioned to Paul, paying no mind to Molly's scowl as she left the kitchen.

A full moon lit the fringe of beach, gilding the tips of breakers moving in on a high tide. Paul seated Suzanne at an umbrella table and remained standing. "Isn't this a sight for the paintbrush?" he said, extending one arm out to the Gulf. "A little different than the Atlantic shore, but we'll be there soon enough. Maybe you'd like to take Suzanne for a stroll on the beach, show her a little of Casey Key while I call Mr. R and pack. How 'bout it, Daniel?"

"Hold on, Paul. You may not need to call Boston just yet. My uncle called here an hour ago. He heard from FBI agent Flynn in Milan. They haven't found the shooter yet, but it's certain the American was killed before he could be extradited. Criminals tend to rat on people when they face jail time. The syndicate acts fast, especially when they lose a million-dollar sale. Flynn assured Uncle that Interpol is cooperating and the painting is on its way."

"We heard the part about the painting, and that makes it easier for me to tell Rafferty that we'll be on our way, too. It wraps things up for us," Paul said.

"Not entirely." Daniel's eyes tracked to Suzanne and back to Paul. "Didn't Detective Canfield speak to you about the break-in?"

Suzanne reached for Paul's hand. "He said he thinks I'm still in danger because they haven't found the intruder."

"And as far as I'm concerned, if we're out of here, we're out of danger," Paul said. He kissed Suzanne's cheek. "Take her for a stroll in the moonlight, Dan. I shouldn't be more than ten minutes getting my belongings together." Paul walked down the hall to his room.

Daniel shook his head. "I don't often play host to ladies here, but I'll do my best. What's your pleasure, Miss Petrone?"

"I'm really not in the mood for a walk, but I wouldn't mind just sticking my toes in the sand out there. It looks like a beautiful vista."

Daniel tried to smile. "Aye, it is, but it's been a long day and a trying one for me, so that's fine. I've also forgotten my manners. Molly would be after me if I didn't offer you refreshment. The beach is just a step outside the door, and I'll bring a glass of wine if you'd like."

Suzanne kicked off her shoes, smiled and nodded. "I'd like that."

Daniel watched her walk gracefully toward the open door before he moved into the kitchen. He threw back a scotch and fixed one for Paul before he poured the wine, all the time glancing out, watching the moonlight shimmer on Suzanne's silhouette. *Good God, it's no wonder . . .* His reverie ended abruptly with the sound of a car pulling into the driveway just as Paul came back into the room. Daniel pointed to the tray of drinks and nodded toward the door. "Take this out to her, Paul. I think we're getting company, and I'm going down to let them in."

Daniel shifted from one foot to the other until the elevator stopped. He opened the garage overhead door and walked directly to the idling car. Detective Canfield had hardly rolled down the passenger window before Daniel spoke. "I don't understand why you're here and not in Bradenton."

Canfield cocked his head to look at Daniel. "I sent a car there as soon as you called. Y'all were timely, and I'm obliged, Kelly. It was close, but an arrest was made."

"I also remembered what you said about meetin' Brant at his favorite bar. The Cove wasn't hard to find down here on the Key. 'Course we knew he wasn't there, but the bartender was very cooperative." For Daniel to see, Canfield held up an evidence bag containing a leather case. He tossed the bag to Maroney.

Daniel pressed his lips together and stepped back when the detective opened the door. As he got out of the car, Detective Canfield pointed back at the case with his thumb. "It could be offered in evidence, but I doubt we need it. According to my boys, Brant came in willingly. I'll be interrogating him soon as we get back. Now if you'll invite me in, I think it's time Miss Petrone knows."

Instead of excitement about packing to leave, Paul dealt with tears after Detective Canfield's disclosure. Granted, it was a shock when he came in and explained about Brant's arrest, but Suzanne's tears were nonstop. She kept saying she didn't understand why he would do such a thing. Paul held her in his arms, trying to soothe her, but her crying unnerved Daniel and eventually brought Molly out of her room.

Daniel explained to Molly as best he could, but no one, least of all Suzanne, understood why Rob Brant would stage a break-in. Molly wasn't easily consoled, either. She simply didn't believe it, and Daniel eventually solved the dilemma by phoning his uncle. Daniel took Molly into his room to make the call.

Rafferty must have smoothed the waters, because Molly came out afterward and gave Paul an Irish blessing for a safe trip home. Daniel said he'd speak to them tomorrow to tell Paul about the call. After hasty farewells, Detective Canfield brought Paul and Suzanne back to Sarasota.

CHAPTER THIRTY-ONE

Daniel hoped this was his last trip to SPD crime division headquarters. Detective Canfield said the arraignment wouldn't happen until Monday, but today being Saturday, Daniel didn't want to wait. He wanted a one-on-one with Rob Brant, and though he didn't advise it, Canfield promised it could happen.

"Why put yourself through it, Kelly?" Canfield told him last night. "The man's in double trouble as it is. He painted the forgery for Scavone. That's aiding and abetting a felony, and next we got him for breaking and entering. There may be more charges, but I doubt Miss Petrone will press. Brant's break-in was a screwy plan from the get-go."

It's that screwy plan I need to hear about, Daniel thought. *Why he did it. . . . I owe that much to Uncle and Paul. I think Rob will tell me.* Daniel entered the building, surprised to see Detective Canfield talking to the desk sergeant. He checked his watch. "You did say I should come at eight A.M.?"

"That's right, but there's been a change of plan. Y'all come upstairs with me, Kelly, and I'll buy you a cup of coffee." Canfield talked all the way up in the elevator. "You won't be able to see Brant today. He had to be transferred to a secure cell downtown late last night."

"Why was that?"

"The man is suicidal."

Daniel stood still at the coffee machine, cup in hand. His face blanched. "What happened? That doesn't sound like the man I knew."

"Come on in and sit, Daniel. It's a side of the man you may never have known. I talked with his sister last night, and she revealed the cause. Her explanation clears up the whole shebang. Robert Brant is a schizophrenic."

"What? I can't believe that."

"I know." Canfield nodded. "Hard to believe. No one suspected when they brought him in, either. He seemed co-operative, even remorseful, but when we came in to interrogate him, he became delusional and agitated. His sister says that happens when he's off his meds or if he mixes the pills with alcohol. She says the disease started when he was a teenager, interfered with college, but your friend had such artistic talent, he wouldn't give up. He's been controlled with medication ever since."

Daniel slowly shook his head. "How could we miss something like that? I mean, the Raffertys, myself, Suzanne. He seemed as normal as you or me."

Canfield nodded his agreement. "That was the Brant you knew. *Seemingly normal.* As I understand it that's the way some schizos are, as long as they take their pills and are stress free. His sister says he's been off his meds since before the hurricane." Canfield turned his attention to Suzanne. "Mister Brant told his sister about you, Miss Petrone. You see, he wanted you to suspect Paul Fontaine of breaking into your apartment to look for the forged painting. He wanted Fontaine out of the picture, you see. He drugged you so you wouldn't know it was really him."

Detective Canfield cocked his head at Daniel. "The gun was just in case his plan didn't work. But I doubt the man would use it. You gottta know, Daniel, that the plan wasn't made by a normal criminal. 'More to be pitied' my Irish mother would say." Canfield shook his head, placing a hand on Daniel's shoulder. "Investigation always has its surprises. I told you the break-in was screwy, but I couldn't make sense of it until last night. Even the best of us don't find all the pieces to a puzzle."

Daniel left headquarters and drove directly to Suzanne's apartment to disclose Canfield's findings. Paul was stunned, but hearing the rest of the story was like salt in the wound. He tried to feel compassion, but being the target for an insane break-in was hard to let go of.

Suzanne was so anguished, she stopped packing. She sat with Daniel, piecing together the times she was in Rob's company, trying to remember anything that might have fed his fantasy. There was no sex. She made that clear from the beginning, yet guilt wouldn't leave her. Rob was a handsome, talented man she thought she could trust. She remembered his delight in any praise she gave him, either for his patience with the students or for his own remarkable talent.

Daniel finally changed the direction of her thoughts. "My uncle said he'd like to meet with you and Paul when your painting arrives at the gallery in Portland. None of this was your fault, Suzanne. You can't make every emotion suspect. Schizophrenia is a disease. My uncle accepted it, and he's a very wise man. He told Molly the most powerful healing tool is forgiveness. It's best you let go of a past that cannot be changed. I learned that from him in Boston when I quit the police force. I had a future waiting to be lived, and so do you."

Paul's smile was wide when Daniel said that. "Yes, she does, and it's going to start today. We have reservations for a two-o'clock flight to Portland. I called a limo service to get us to Tampa, and we'll be out of your hair permanently, Daniel."

"You didn't get in my hair. I shared a lot with you, Paul." Daniel's mouth twitched, and his blue eyes sparked in a rare smile. "Even my Mozart," he said, his eyebrows lifting with a nod of his head. "But I have to admit this investigation had its lessons, too, working with Canfield, eh?"

"He's a rare bird, for sure," Paul said.

Daniel shook Paul's hand. "Aye, but he's the best. As he would say, y'all come see us at Seaview, sometime, ya hear?"

The mandatory hour before departure left time to kill, so Paul and Suzanne ate lunch at the airport. They had just finished when Paul's cell phone rang. A glance at the readout brought relief. "Hi again, *Tante* Margaret. I just spoke to you this morning. What's up?"

"I forgot to ask you something for Clare. She wants to know if she and Remi can meet your plane and bring you down to your papa's."

"That's a nice offer, but it won't be necessary, *Tante*." Paul reached for Suzanne's hand. "Tell Clare thanks, but we're going to have a late supper at DiMillo's in Old Port, and we may stay in Portland till tomorrow."

After a pause Margaret said, "Tomorrow is Sunday, Jacques Paul. Everyone is coming to the house so we can talk about the wedding after mass."

"Mass at Mary Star of the Sea chapel?"

"*Oui.* You didn't give me time to tell you that plans have changed for Clare and Remi. Jamie Windspirit is still in remission, but they are doing some new radiation therapy, and Remi thinks it's too much for his parents to have the reception at the inn. So, the wedding will be here at the chapel, and the reception will be at Francois's Fancy. The wedding is a week from today, Jacques Paul."

"Whoa! I mean, it sounds great, but is this all okay with Pa?"

"It's fine with Jacques, *oui*. He is happy to give my Clare away, and he is anxious to meet your Suzanne. So is everyone. *Moi aussi.* Will you please come tonight?"

"Uh . . . I'm renting a car at the airport, and I guess we could drive down after supper." Paul raised a questioning eyebrow at Suzanne. She nodded, checked her watch and picked up her carry-on. "It will be late, but we'll be there. They're calling our departure, so I gotta go, now. Love you, Auntie Mame."

Jacques and *Tante* Margaret were waiting when Paul drove into Francois's Fancy. Margaret stood in the open kitchen door. "*Mére de Dieu,* you are a feast for the eyes!" Tante said.

Paul put their overnight bags down, laughing. He kissed Margaret's cheek and walked into his father's open arms. "It's good to be home, Pa." He reached for Suzanne's hand. "I guess you know I brought a guest with me. Suzanne Petrone, meet my father, Jacques, and the other special lady in my life, *Tante* Margaret."

Jacques took Suzanne's hand in both of his. "It's a pleasure to welcome you, my dear."

Margaret watched Paul limp toward the luggage. "How is your hip, *cherie?* No more cane, eh?"

"No, no cane. My leg's doing better, but I think I'll leave these by the stairs." He handed one bag to Margaret. "Shall we go in and sit down, Pa? I want to hear about your surgery. What does the doc have to say?"

Jacques put his hand to his throat. "It's healing nicely, and I have few restrictions. Margaret has taken good care of me. She'll be here until Wednesday, and then Kathleen will be coming home, just in time for the wedding."

"You're sure it's not going to be too much for you, Pa? How big a wedding is it?"

"Only thirty people, Jacques Paul," Margaret answered. "Some of Clare and Remi's work friends and the Windspirit and Donovan families. They wanted to keep it small, and Clare is having a caterer, so everything will be okay, eh, Jacques?"

"The wedding plans are fine, and you'll hear all about them tomorrow, I'm sure, but I'm anxious to hear about the painting, Paul." Jacques looked from Margaret to Paul. "I know it's late, but Margaret only told us that the stolen painting was found in Italy."

Paul looked at Suzanne and squeezed her hand. "For now, that's all that is important, Pa. The forged painting appearing in Florida was a hoax designed to allow criminals to take the stolen painting overseas. The FBI brought the real Monet back, and it will be on its way to the gallery this week."

Jacques shook his head. "Looks like you've crossed the Rubicon, Paul." Jacques cocked his head toward Suzanne. "But what an ordeal that must have been for you, my dear."

Suzanne nodded. "Yes, but Paul helped me get through it all, Mr. Fontaine."

"Sean Rafferty will be meeting us at the gallery when the Monet arrives, so Suzanne and I will be going up to Portland tomorrow night to stay until Friday."

Margaret stood. "You must be tired, Jacques Paul. Both of you." She turned her gaze to Suzanne. "I think we all need a good night's rest for tomorrow, eh? Maddy's room is all ready for Suzanne."

"I thought you were staying in Maddy's room, *Tante*," Paul said.

"*Oui*, I was, but we opened up the back bedroom this morning."

"Good Lord, that hasn't been used since Grandpa Frank died."

"I know, but I gave it a good cleaning. I will sleep in peace no matter where I am, and your papa will, too, now that you are home, *mon cherie*."

Paul waited in the open door of Maddy's room until Jacques and *Tante* had gone to their bedrooms. He pulled Suzanne into his arms. "Can't buck the plans tonight, my sweet, but tomorrow night will be ours." He kissed her tenderly. "What do you think of Pa and *Tante?*"

"I think your father is a dear, and *Tante*"—Suzanne smiled and snuggled into his shoulder—"I think she is a very wise woman."

Everyone came to Francois's Fancy directly after early mass. Four cars filled the driveway all the way around to the side door. Remi and Clare, Maddy and Patrick followed Paul around the cars and up onto the porch. "Suzanne is in already with *Tante* and Pa, and he insists you come around to the front. Margaret had things set up on the porch before we went to church. It was such a beautiful June morning, Suzanne and I took a sunrise walk on the beach, while *Tante* set things up."

Clare squeezed Paul's arm. "I told you my mom takes over. I hope she doesn't scare Suzanne. She's a beauty, Paul. How did you keep her a secret so long?"

"Never underestimate your mom, babe. *Tante* is a keeper of secrets and promises, and Suzanne really admires her."

Maddy turned and whispered, "Shh, here they come."

Jacques held the screen door open, and Margaret led Suzanne out, both carrying trays. "Suzanne has mimosas and I have Irish coffee," *Tante* said. "Take your choice and then, my darlings Clare and Remi, you will tell us all the plans."

"Not a lot is different," Clare said. "The priest agreed to the change two weeks ago, and luckily the chapel could accommodate us. Remi wants his dad for best man. And of course, Maddy is my maid of honor."

"Patrick and Paul will usher, but not to worry. No tuxes this time, guys," Remi said. "Rehearsal is at the chapel Friday, and dinner will be at the inn afterward. My mom insisted she wants to do that."

"Aren't you forgetting something?" Maddy asked, turning her eyes to *Tante*.

"Never, ever," Clare said. "I was sure Paul knows that my mom will be at Papa Jacques's side to give me away."

"I did know about that," Paul said. "Pa and I talked a little about your wedding this morning, and about other things." Paul looked at his father, and Jacques nodded, smiling. "I was going to wait until your wedding was over to tell everyone about our talk, but then I remembered your wedding day is also Remi's birthday, and you will have plenty to celebrate. So I guess the time is right today."

Paul pulled a small box out of his pocket, and flashed a smile to Maddy. He took a deep breath, closed his eyes and wiped a tear away. "Pa gave this to me just before we went to church. It was Mom's engagement ring." He quickly turned to Suzanne with the diamond. "She's already said yes," he said as he slipped the ring on her finger.

Everyone jumped up at once and crowded in to kiss Suzanne and congratulate Paul. *Tante* Margaret was the last to join the circle.

She grasped both their hands. *"C'est incroyable, mon chèries."*

"You're right *Tante*, it is incredible." He kissed first *Tante*'s cheek and then Suzanne's. "Two of my lady loves. You won't have to worry about my head in the crow's nest, anymore, *Tante*." He drew Suzanne close. "With my first mate by my side, my feet will be firmly planted on the deck from now on."

ABOUT THE AUTHOR

Doctor **Mary Fremont Schoenecker** took early retirement from teaching at State University of New York to live with husband, Tom, in southwest Florida. Mother of four grown children and grandmother of fourteen, Mary's debut historical novel, *Four Summers Waiting* depicted real ancestors of her children in an epic story of the Civil War. Her second book, *Finding Fiona,* was the first installment in a contemporary series, *Maine Shore Chronicles.* Book Two of the Chronicles, *Moonglade,* was published by Five Star in 2010. *Promise Keeper* is Book Three in the series. Read more about Mary on her Web site, www.maryschoenecker.com.